THE MILK MAID ORPHAN

CATHARINE DOBBS

Copyright © 2024 by Catharine Dobbs

All rights reserved.

No part of this book may be reproduced in any form or by any electronic or mechanical means, including information storage and retrieval systems, without written permission from the author, except for the use of brief quotations in a book review.

PROLOGUE

THE MILKMAID

Wales, Winter, 1855

"That's right, not too much. We don't want to kill anyone, Cadell," his father said, watching as Cadell add handfuls of chalk to the churn of milk his cousin had just brought from the milking shed.

"What if Mother knew about this?" Cadell Parry replied, looking up at his father with an uncertain look.

He did not like the idea of adding chalk to the milk. It seemed wrong–it was wrong. But his father merely cuffed him around the ear.

"She won't know about it, Cadell. I'm doing it for her– I'm doing it for all of you. We've got more mouths to feed now. The milk isn't worth anything on its own. No...

there's no choice. Do you think I like doing it? No... but the ends justify the means. Now, add the chalk," he snarled, and Cadell nodded, taking a handful of chalk, and dropping it into the milk...

IT WAS STILL DARK when Gwen Parry made her way to the milking shed. But she was used to the early rising, to the dark mornings–except in summer, when she awoke with the first rays of dawn. But in the depths of winter, with the snow lying thick on the bleak hillside and the farm shrouded in a blanket of darkness, she shivered, pulling her shawl tightly around her shoulders.

"Bluebell are you awake?" she called out, holding up a lamp above the stall, where the heifer was lying amidst the hay.

A low mooing was the reply, and the animal rose to its feet, reluctant, just as Gwen had been, to be awoken at such a time. But such was the life of a milkmaid, and at just seven years old, it was the only life Gwen had ever known. Her aunt and uncle owned Talfryn Farm, a hill farm in the depths of the Welsh valleys, where the dairy herd provided a livelihood of milk, some of it sent to London on the stream train, and some made into butter and cheese and sold at the local market. Gwen had lived with her aunt and uncle since she was very young, and she knew of no other life but this.

"Come along, Bluebell. It's time for your milking. Uncle's bringing in the others now," Gwen said.

Bluebell had not been well, but she had made a good recovery and was due to be returned to the herd that day. Gwen's uncle had instructed her to milk the heifer before he brought the rest of the herd in, and now she took a bucket and a milking stool as Bluebell stood waiting patiently.

Gwen could not remember learning to milk. She had always known how to do so, and now she sat, lost in thought, as she gently teased the milk from Bluebell's udders.

"There now, you can rest again soon," she whispered, stroking the animals' side.

She spoke to all the cattle as though they could understand her. Each had their own ways, and she had a name for each of them—Bluebell, Clover, Daisy, Dandelion... Gwen was trying to teach the names to her sister, but Madlen was too young to remember them, and she would merely repeat them without referring to a specific animal.

"Gwen are you finished with Bluebell?" a voice from outside the milking shed called out.

It was her Uncle Dawid, returned with the rest of the herd, and Gwen hurried to finish, knowing she would be in trouble if she dallied.

"I'm coming, Uncle," she called out, patting Bluebell and taking the bucket of warm milk from beneath her.

Outside, the air was even colder than in the milkshed,

and in the first rays of dawn, Gwen could see the plumes of breath from the herd rising in the still air. Her uncle was waiting for her.

"Quickly, Gwen. Take that milk into the dairy, then go and check on your aunt. But I want you back out here to see to the cattle–they all need milking," her uncle said.

Gwen nodded. Her aunt had been unwell for the past few weeks–a fever confining her to her bed. It had meant a great deal more work for Gwen, who had had to act as mother to her brother and sister and take on her aunt's duties around the farm. She was only seven years old, but the burdens of her responsibility were great, and now she made way into the farmhouse, where a solitary lamp burned in the parlour. Her cousin, Cadell, was sitting by the hearth toasting a piece of bread on a toasting fork, and he looked up at Gwen and sneered.

"Shouldn't you be milking?" he said.

Cadell was ten years old, but behaved as though the farm was already his, lauding it over Gwen and her sister, and treating her brother Owain as his prodigy.

"I've come to check on Aunt Cerian. She didn't have a good night," Gwen said, taking the kettle and hanging it on a hook over the grate.

Gwen had been awake for most of the night tending to her aunt, whose fever had taken a turn for the worse. She was suffering badly, and the doctor had been sent for, even as he had told them, there was little he could do but hope for the best.

"Keep her warm, make sure she drinks plenty of hot tea," he had said, leaving a foul-smelling tonic for Gwen to administer.

"Check on her, then get back out to the milking. I've got to see to the pigs," Cadell said.

He spoke with an authority far beyond his years, and when his father was absent, he behaved as though his inheritance was certain. Gwen ignored him. She made tea in the pot and sliced some bread, spreading it with damson jam to tempt her aunt into eating.

Placing the breakfast on a tray, she made her way up the narrow staircase to the upper rooms of the farmhouse. It was an ancient dwelling, a narrow house, fortified at one end with a small peel tower, now largely in ruins. The family occupied the end half of the house, and Gwen slept with her sister, who now appeared in the doorway of the stairs leading to their attic room.

"Aunt Cerian is crying," she said, and Gwen shooed her back to bed.

"I'll see to her. But you'll catch a fever, too, if you stand there in just your nightgown, Madlen. Get dressed, then you can help with the milking," Gwen replied.

Her aunt's bedroom was at the far end of the corridor, and Gwen knocked gently at the door, listening for her aunt's reply.

"Gwen... is that you?" her aunt called out, her voice weak and feeble.

"It is, Aunt Cerian, yes. I've brought you some tea," Gwen said, opening the door cautiously.

The wintry early morning sunlight was coming through the window, and she found her aunt in bed, covered by several blankets. She had once been a strong and sturdy farmer's wife, with rosy, red cheeks, and a booming voice. But the fever had reduced her to a mere shadow of her former self, her face pale and pinched, her frame hunched beneath the blankets. She tried to sit up, groaning as she did so—the fever was taking its toll.

"Gwen... oh, Gwen..." she said, as Gwen set down the tray on the bedside table and tried to help her aunt sit up in bed.

"It's alright, Aunt Cerian. I can help you," Gwen said, but she struggled to help her aunt sit up, and though she tried her best, she could only manage to prop the pillows up before holding the cup of tea for her aunt to drink.

"I'm sorry, Gwen, I'm sorry," her aunt said, but Gwen shook her head.

Her aunt had nothing to be sorry for. She had taken her and her brother and sister in when their mother had died, and their father had abandoned them. She had been a mother to Gwen, caring for her, and giving her a home. Gwen loved her aunt dearly, and it brought tears to her eyes to see her reduced to such a state.

"It's alright, Aunt Cerian. I'm here," Gwen said.

"You'll get into trouble with your uncle if you stay. He'll want you to milk the cows. How was Bluebell *today?" her aunt asked, for she was always concerned about the herd.*

The farm had belonged to Gwen's aunt's family for six generations, and she had lived there her whole life long. The herd was hers, descended through the ages, but times were hard, and it was proving ever more difficult to turn a profit.

The price of milk was going down, and the cost of keeping the herd was going up. The sale of butter and cheese brought some income, but with her aunt ill, its production was lessened, and the dairy was in disarray.

"She's better, yes. She's ready to go back with the herd. Uncle Dawid just brought them round from the barn. But he can wait," Gwen replied, *for she did not want to leave her aunt alone, not when she was so ill.*

The fever had her in its grip. She was growing worse, and Gwen feared for what would become of her–and them.

"Poor Gwen, my dear girl. You mustn't let your uncle... oh, the farm... the herd... it's all over, isn't it?" her aunt said, *lying back on the pillows with a sigh.*

"You'll get better, Aunt Cerian, I promise," Gwen said, *but her aunt shook her head.*

"I'm drifting away, Gwen. I can feel it. Little by little," she said, *reaching out to take Gwen's hand in hers.*

"Won't you eat something?" Gwen asked, *but her aunt shook her head.*

"I don't want anything... just... to rest," she said, and Gwen nodded.

Her aunt closed her eyes, still holding Gwen's hand in hers. For a moment, Gwen watched her, and it seemed as though the life was slipping from her. She stepped forward, concerned, even as a voice came calling out from below.

"Gwen, I need you outside. There's milking to do," her uncle called out.

But Gwen did not respond. Her aunt's hand was limp, her eyes closed, her head resting to the side. She was gone. Tears welled up in Gwen's eyes, and she squeezed her aunt's hand, imploring her to wake up.

"Aunt Cerian," she said, but there was no response.

The door of her aunt's bedroom opened, and her uncle appeared with an angry look on his face.

"Gwen, those cows won't milk themselves. Get out there," he snarled, but Gwen turned to him, shaking her aunt.

"She's gone, Uncle," she said, as tears rolled down her cheeks.

PART I

THE VALLEY

"God has her in His care, Dawid," the minister said, and Gwen's uncle nodded.

"I know that Reverend, but it doesn't make it any easier to live with. She was a good woman, a good wife and mother," he said, shaking his head.

News of the death of Gwen's aunt had spread quickly through the valley. It was a close-knit community, where everyone knew everyone else, and the chapel was at its heart. Reverend Tobias Llewelyn had come at once, and prayers had been said, along with the reading of scripture.

Gwen sat with Madlen and Owain by the hearth, and Cadell sat next to his father at the table. The body of Gwen's aunt was still upstairs, covered with a pall, and the minister was discussing the arrangements for the funeral.

"And she'll be remembered as such, Dawid. It'll be a dignified funeral, a fitting tribute," the minister said, and Gwen's uncle nodded.

On discovering his wife's death, he had broken down, collapsing to the floor in a fit of sobs. Gwen had never seen such a side of him, and she had done her best to comfort him. He could be a cruel man, but the death of Gwen's aunt had overwhelmed him, and now he sat at the table, staring into the distance, despairing, it seemed, of what was to come.

"She meant everything to me," Gwen's uncle said, and Reverend Llewelyn nodded.

"I know she did, Dawid. But you must be strong–for the sake of the children, you must be strong. And the farm," he said.

Gwen's uncle glanced at her, shaking his head as tears rolled down his cheeks.

"How am I supposed to look after them? The farm, a family... I can't do it," he said, but the minister shook his head.

"With God's grace, Dawid–that's how. Don't think about it now. You're consumed by your grief. But it'll get easier. By God's grace, it'll get easier," he replied.

Gwen's aunt had been a devout chapel goer, and she had raised the children–her own son, and Gwen and her brother and sister–the same. Every Sunday, they would make their way down the valley path from the farm to the chapel, joined by their friends and neighbours.

There, they would sing hymns of praise to God and listen to Reverend Llewelyn's sermon. Grace would be said before meals, and Gwen and the others were always made to kneel at their bedside before going to sleep to say their prayers.

"We thank God for the day, and ask for protection in the night," her aunt would say.

Now, Gwen could only hope her aunt's faithfulness was rewarded, just as Reverend Llewelyn said it was. Their lives were shaped by this hope, but it did not seem to make Gwen's grief any easier to bear. She missed her aunt terribly and wanted only to weep at her loss.

"I hope you're right, Reverend Llewelyn," Gwen's uncle said.

"Cadell, take the children outside. I want to talk to your father alone," the minister said.

Cadell began to object, but his father gave him a stern look.

"Do as you're told, Cadell. For once, do as you're told," he snarled, and Cadell fell silent.

He pointed to Gwen, indicating for her to usher Owain and Madlen out of the parlour. The day was cold, but bright, and they stood together in the farmyard, looking out over the valley. Gwen had seen to the milking herself, but the herd was still in the milking shed, waiting to be led back to the barn.

Cadell turned on Gwen angrily.

"If you'd taken better care of her, she wouldn't have died," he snarled, raising his hand as though to strike Gwen around the face.

She drew back, her eyes filled with tears, shaking her head as she faced her cousin defiantly.

"She had a fever, Cadell. You know that. And what did you do for her? Nothing. You never once offered to sit with her or nurse her. You never took her a tray or offered to help me. I did everything I could for her. I know you're angry, but… we're all upset," she said, and Madlen now began to cry.

Gwen put her arms around her to comfort her. She was only three years old and did not understand what had happened, but knew something was wrong, and her sobs echoed around the farmyard as Gwen lifted her into her arms.

"I had my own responsibilities. You were supposed to look after her," Cadell snarled, but Gwen had heard enough.

"Come along Madlen, come along, Owain, we'll go and see Bluebell," Gwen said, trying to hold back her tears for the sake of the others.

But Cadell snatched Owain's hand and pulled

him away. He was five years old and followed Cadell around like a puppy.

"Owain's coming with me," Cadell said, leading Owain away.

Madlen clung to Gwen, who shook her head and sighed, carrying her sister into the milking shed, where the herd was waiting patiently to be returned to the barn. Bluebell was sitting in her stall, and Gwen put Madlen down, brushing the tears from her eyes. She had done everything she could for her aunt, and it was a cruel and heartless thing to suggest otherwise.

"Do you understand what's happened, Madlen?" Gwen asked.

Her sister was stroking Bluebell's nose, and she looked up at Gwen and shook her head.

"Everyone is crying," she said, and Gwen nodded.

"Because Aunt Cerian's gone to heaven," she said.

She did not entirely understand it herself. But Reverend Llewelyn had assured her of the fact, and Gwen knew her aunt had believed the same.

"When we die, we go to heaven," she had often told Gwen.

It was a fact, just as the sky was blue, and the cows needed milking. Madlen thought for a moment.

"Then why is everyone sad? Isn't heaven nice?" she asked, and Gwen sighed.

"It is, yes. But we're sad because we miss Aunt Cerian," she said.

Again, Madlen thought for a moment.

"I miss her," she said, and Gwen nodded.

"I miss her, too, Madlen," she replied, wondering what would become of her and her brother and sister now.

Gwen's uncle had made no secret of his opposition to Gwen, Owain, and Madlen coming to live at Talfryn Farm. He complained about mouths to feed and costs to bear. But Gwen's aunt had been adamant in her intention to take care of the three children, and she had treated them as her own.

"I love you just as if I'd born you myself, Gwen," she had once said, and Gwen had always felt loved and wanted by her aunt, even as her uncle could be cruel.

But what would become of them now was an open question. Gwen's uncle could not hope to run the farm himself, but nor would he want responsibility for four children, three of whom were not his own.

"We've got to work hard, Madlen. You'll have to help me with the milking. And Owain, too. We'll have to earn our keep," Gwen said, fearing their uncle would use any excuse to be rid of them.

Gwen had heard stories about the orphanage in the town beyond the valley, where children without parents were sent, and life was harsh and unforgiving. She had come to love Talfryn Farm, and its rolling pastures and green meadows.

The valley was idyllic, with its soaring hills, lush woodlands, and gushing streams. Gwen knew every inch of it, and she could not imagine being anywhere else but within its confines.

"I'll have to help?" Madlen asked, looking down at Bluebell, who was chewing on a piece of straw.

"That's right. We've got to work hard and help Uncle Dawid," she said.

Madlen nodded, running her hand along the heifer's nose and smiling. She did not understand what had happened, even as Gwen had tried her best to explain it. But with their aunt gone, life for Gwen and Madlen would be harder, that much was certain, and her uncle's voice called out across the farmyard, demanding to know where she was, Gwen knew the coming days and weeks would not be easy.

THE DAY of the funeral was bleak and cold. A blanket of snow covered the valley, and as the funeral procession made its slow way down the track from the farm, Gwen could not hold back her tears.

The coffin was carried by the farm labourers, young men, wearing black armbands, wrapped in overcoats against the cold. It was led by Reverend Llewelyn, wearing a white surplice over his black preaching gown, reciting verses of scripture as they went. Gwen walked behind her uncle and cousin, holding Madlen's hand, and Owain walked in front of them.

"I said, I will take heed to my ways: that I offend not in my tongue. I will keep my mouth as it were with a bridle while the ungodly is in my sight. I held my tongue, and spake nothing: I kept silence, yea, even from good words; but it was pain and grief for me. My heart was hot within me, and while I was thus musing the fire kindled: and at the last I spake with my tongue; Lord, let me know mine end, and the number of my days: that I may be certified how long I have to live…" Reverend Llewelyn's words echoed across the valley, accompanied by the slow march of the procession's footsteps.

Many of their neighbours had turned out to accompany the coffin to its final resting place, and by the time they had arrived at the chapel–a brick building with an arched roof, surrounded by yew trees and half fallen gravestones–a sizable crowd had gathered.

It was snowing now, and the wind was bitter. Madlen clung to Gwen, who was wrapped in two shawls, one of which had belonged to her aunt.

"Are you ready, Dawid?" the minister asked, turning to Gwen's uncle, who nodded.

"Let's get this over with," he replied, ushering Cadell into the chapel.

Gwen was left with her brother and sister, and the crowd now followed her uncle inside, jostling for seats as the coffin was brought to the front of the chapel, its whitewashed walls and plain glass windows emphasising the stark nature of death. It was lit only by candlelight, the flames flickering in the dim afternoon light. Reverend Llewelyn now stood at the front, and Gwen, Owain, and Madlen were ushered into one of the pews near the front.

"I am the resurrection and the life, saith the Lord: he that believeth in me, though he were dead, yet shall he live and whosoever liveth and believeth in me shall never die," the minister said, and the funeral service began.

Reverend Llewelyn gave a short eulogy, extolling Gwen's aunt as an example of the Christian life and praising her for her kindness in taking in the children of her dead sister.

"In this, as in so many ways, she is an example to us all," he said.

A tear rolled down Gwen's cheek. She missed her aunt terribly. In the past week, dozens of people had come to the farm to pay their respects. Her aunt had been well liked and respected in the valley, and there were many who mourned her.

When the funeral service came to an end, the coffin was born by the bearers out into the graveyard, where the grave had been dug in the far corner, below the wall. The snow was drifting there, and it took some time for the congregation to gather for the burial.

Madlen was shivering, and Gwen picked her up as best she could, wrapping her in her shawl as the coffin was lowered into the ground.

"Forasmuch as it hath pleased Almighty God of his great mercy to take unto himself the soul of our dear brother here departed: we therefore commit his body to the ground; earth to earth, ashes to ashes, dust to dust; in sure and certain hope of the Resurrection to eternal life…" Reverend Llewelyn intoned, pronouncing the words of committal over the grave before tossing a handful of dirt onto the coffin below.

The wind moaned through the trees, and Madlen began to cry, clinging to Gwen, who was sobbing, too. Gwen's uncle wept, but Cadell remained stoic, standing at his mother's graveside, as the snow fell around them.

The rest of the congregation did not remain for long, and when the minister had pronounced the final blessing, they dispersed. Gwen was left with

Madlen in her arms, and her uncle now turned, not saying a word as he strode past her.

Cadell followed, pushing Owain along with him, leaving Gwen and Madlen at the graveside.

"I miss her," Madlen said.

"I miss her, too," Gwen replied, as now the gravedigger came hurrying over.

"I need to be quick–can't have the snow filling it instead," he said, shovelling the first spade full of earth onto the coffin lid.

Gwen did not want to watch, turning away, even as she felt guilty for leaving her aunt alone in the graveyard. But the forgotten graves around them spoke of a similar testimony. Birth and death, life given, then forgotten.

"But we won't forget Aunt Cerian, will we, Madlen?" Gwen said, and her sister shook her head.

"I liked her smile," she said, and Gwen nodded.

"I liked it, too," Gwen replied, remembering her aunt's smiling face, with its rosy cheeks and bright blue eyes.

She had never heard her speak ill of anyone, and the only time she spoke a cross word was when she burned the griddle cakes, chastising herself for doing so. She had been their mother, and it was as a mother they would mourn her.

"I'm cold, Gwen," Madlen said, shivering in Gwen's arms.

"Then let's go back to the farm. I'll make you some hot tea," Gwen said, setting her sister down and taking her by the hand.

Her uncle and cousin were already striding ahead, followed by Owain, who was struggling to keep up. Gwen was worried about her brother. Cadell treated him as his own, and wherever he went, Owain followed. He was under Cadell's influence, and in the days since his mother's death, Cadell had become ever crueller and angrier.

"Will you carry me?" Madlen asked, but she was getting too big to be carried, and Gwen had to coax her along, promising her hot toasted muffins to go with her tea.

But when they arrived back at the farm, they found their uncle waiting for them.

"See to the herd, Gwen. They need to go back in the barn. Take your sister with you," he snarled, before she had even stepped over the threshold into the parlour.

"But Uncle Dawid, we're both so cold. Can't we warm ourselves by the fire? I was going to make Madlen some tea, and I promised her toasted muffins and butter," Gwen said, but her uncle glared at her angrily.

"The cows won't see to themselves, Gwen. The sooner you get them into the barn, the sooner you can sit in front of the hearth, though why I should allow it, I don't know. Your aunt indulged you–tea, toasted muffins? You need to start paying your way, Gwen. There's work to do," he replied, pointing back out into the darkening afternoon.

Cadell smirked from his place by the fire. He had Owain at his feet, and Gwen looked at her brother imploringly. But there was no doubting where his loyalties lay, and he merely looked up at Gwen with an innocent expression on his face.

"Yes, Uncle," Gwen replied, taking Madlen by the hand.

"But I'm cold," Madlen said, as she followed Gwen outside.

It was nearly dark now, and the task of getting the cows back into the barn would be made far harder by the lack of light. Gwen opened the door of the milking shed, calling out to the cows to follow her, and making Madlen stand back lest she be trampled.

The air was filled with the lowing of the cattle, and Gwen coaxed them out into the farmyard, opening the barn doors to usher them inside. But it was far harder in the dark, and several of the animals went their own way, jostling with one another, as Gwen tried desperately to control them.

"This way, not over there… oh, please… won't you do as you're told," she exclaimed, pushing at the cattle, and trying to steer them towards the barn.

Madlen started to cry, and Gwen picked her up, setting her on an upturned bucket next to Bluebell.

"You look after Bluebell, and don't move," Gwen said, stepping back out of the milking shed to find the cattle having dispersed in every direction around the farmyard.

It took an hour or more to get all of them into the barn, and when she and Madlen returned to the warmth of the parlour, their hands were blue with cold.

"What took you so long?" her uncle growled.

He was sitting by the fire, eating bread and cheese. Cadell had an empty plate in his hand, and the remnants of a fruit cake lay on the table. Owain was fast asleep on the rug in front of the fire, lying curled up with one of the dogs. Madlen began to cry.

"It takes longer in the dark. She's cold. She needs something to eat," Gwen said.

"Then make her some tea and toast some bread. There's the end of the loaf there," Gwen's uncle said, pointing to the crusts left on the table.

Cadell smirked.

"I'm going to have the last piece of cake," he said, snatching it before either Gwen or Madlen could share it between them.

Gwen sighed. There was no point in arguing. She made the tea, glad, at least, of the warmth of the cup in her hand, and having toasted the last of the bread, she gave Gwen the bigger piece, spread with dripping.

Life had changed in so many ways since the death of her aunt, and Gwen knew it would only get harder, even as she knew she had no choice but to do as she was told or suffer the consequences.

THE DAIRY HERD

*S*pring came late to Talfryn Farm that year, the winter proving long and hard. But with the thaw came a sense of hope, and despite her troubles, Gwen could look forward to warmer days, and the prospect of summer ahead.

She loved to watch the valley come to life after its winter sleep. The wildflowers blooming in the hedgerows, the birds returning from their far-off travels, the first of the lambs born in the pastures…

"It feels like a happy time," Gwen thought to herself.

But with the thaw came a new set of demands, and the work of the farm continued unceasingly. The calving season had arrived, and new arrivals for the herd meant extra work. Bluebell was expecting, as were many of the others, and Gwen was kept busy taking care of them and watching for the signs of imminent arrivals.

"It'll be any day now for some of them," her uncle said, sending Gwen out to the field one morning in late April.

He had continued to treat Gwen and her sister harshly. They rose before dawn and did not go to bed until late at night. Not only was Gwen expected to see to her tasks on the farm, but she was also expected to take care of the house, and she would cook and clean, keep the fires going, mend and sew, wash and iron. Her uncle was relentless in his demands, reminding her every day of the debt she owed him.

"You're here because of charity, Gwen. You aunt took you in, not me," he would say, whenever she dared to question his orders.

Gwen had learned to keep quiet, not complaining, and doing as she was told. Her only friend was Madlen, who had learned to help as much as she could. But as for Owain, his loyalties had been decided. He was Cadell's through and through, always following him around following his cousin's orders.

It saddened Gwen to see it, but there was nothing she could do to break her brother's misplaced loyalty. Cadell had him in his power, and whilst Gwen had tried her best to prevent his influence, the damage was done.

"Get out and see to the herd, Gwen–you know it won't be long for Bluebell," Cadell said, mimicking his father, who had gone out to see to the pigs.

"Yes, Gwen, do as you're told," Owain said, laughing as Cadell pushed Gwen roughly towards the farmhouse door.

"It's you that should do as you're told, Owain," Gwen said, and she reached out and cuffed her younger brother around the ear.

Cadell grabbed hold of her hand, twisting her wrist, and Gwen let out a cry of pain. Madlen was standing next to her, and she began beating at Cadell's legs with her fists, even as he pushed her away.

"You don't tell Owain what to do, do you hear me?" he snarled, pushing Gwen towards the door.

She fell to the floor, the hard flagstone jarring her knees, and she scrambled to her feet, fighting back the tears, and not wishing to give him the satisfaction of seeing her upset. Madlen ran to her side, and Gwen took her sister's hand, leading her out into the farmyard, as the sounds of Owain laughing with his cousin came from inside.

"Why is Owain so nasty?" Madlen said as they

made their way towards the gate leading to the meadows.

"Because he's been taught to be nasty by a nasty person, Madlen. Don't ever forget how easy it is to learn hatred," Gwen said.

Her brother had been a sweet little boy, very affectionate, but Cadell had turned him, like sour milk. He would grow up the same way, and Gwen was fearful of what life would be like when the two boys came of age.

"I wish he was nice. I wish Cadell was nice, too," Madlen said, taking Gwen's hand in hers.

"I wish he was, too. But he's only got worse since Aunt Cerian died," Gwen replied, shaking her head sadly.

But the sight of the meadows bursting with wildflowers cheered her mood. The cows had been let out to pasture after the thaw, and Gwen could see Bluebell in the far corner, eating the grass. They made their way through the herd, checking on the pregnant heifers as they went. Many of them were close to giving birth, interspersed with the older cows, whose only function was now milk and eventually meat.

The herd was ever changing, the older animals slaughtered, and new ones born to replace them. As they approached, Bluebell looked up and let out a loud moo. Gwen reached out and stroked her nose.

"She's very close, isn't she?" Madlen said, running her hand along the bulk of Bluebell's stomach.

Gwen nodded. She had often watched her uncle calving, and she knew how to tell when a heifer was close to giving birth. Bluebell would have her calf soon, that much was certain, and Gwen intended to be there with her, stroking her nose and doing what she could to make the animal comfortable.

"We'll tell Uncle Dawid when we get back. But he'll want the milkers now. I'm surprised Cadell hasn't come out already," Gwen said.

Along with herself, there were three labourers on the farm–men who lived above one of the barns and worked in the milking shed. They would help transport the milk churns down to the railway, where they would be loaded onto carriages for the journey out of the valley and on to London.

It had always amazed Gwen to think of the milk the herd produced finding its way to the bustling streets of the capital. Gwen had never left the valley, and she could only imagine what the world beyond was like.

"Here's Aled now," Madlen said, pointing across the meadow as one of the labourers approached the gate from the farmyard.

He waved to Gwen and her sister, opening the gate, and calling to the milkers to follow him. The cows had a way of knowing when it was time for them to be milked, and they plodded across the field, making their way slowly into the farmyard. Some had bells hung around their necks, and the familiar dingle echoed back across the meadow.

"He'll want us to help. Come along, Madlen, we don't want to get into trouble," Gwen said, beckoning her younger sister to follow her.

Madlen did so, and the two of them followed the herd into the farmyard. Aled was slapping the rumps of the cows, driving them towards the milking shed, and Cadell and Owain now appeared at the farmhouse door.

"Hurry up, Aled, we need to get the churns ready for the cart," Cadell called out.

Aled, a tall, lanky boy of sixteen, caught Gwen's eye and smiled. He was used to Cadell lauding it over the farm, even as he could easily have put him across his knee.

"Yes, Master Cadell," he called out, with a slight imitation of Gwen's cousin's shrill voice.

Gwen liked Aled. He never raised his voice or ordered her about. But he, too, was often on the receiving end of Gwen's uncle's anger, and now he had no choice but to do as he was told, hurrying the last of the cows towards the milking shed, as Gwen fetched a stool and a bucket.

It would take the rest of the afternoon to milk the cows, then she would be expected to see to the task in the house–preparing a meal for her uncle and Cadell, and finish darning the shirts she was mending for them.

"Take a stool, too, Madlen. You're nearly big enough to do it on your own now," Gwen said, beckoning her sister to help.

Madlen wanted to help, but she was not yet big enough to handle a cow on her own, and she sat next to Gwen, watching as she drew the milk down from the udders into the bucket. Aled was humming to himself. He had a good voice and sang in the chapel choir. It pleased Gwen to hear him sing–hymns and valley songs, his voice strong and clear.

"Sing the one about the blackbird," Madlen said, and Aled looked up from his milking and smiled.

"That's your favourite, isn't it, Madlen?" he said, and Madlen nodded, as Aled began to sing.

"Blackbird, you who travels my lands,
Oh, you who know the old and new,
Will you give counsel to a young lad
Who has been pining for more than a year?

"Oh, come closer, lad, and listen,
To find out what ails you,
When either the world turns against you,
Or you pine for someone's love."

Oh, it's not the world that turns against me,
Nor do I pine for someone's love,
But I see the fair girls becoming scarce
I don't know where to turn for love."

"What's all this noise?" a voice from outside demanded, and the door of the milking shed was pulled open, and Gwen's uncle looked in with an angry expression on his face.

"I'm sorry, sir, I was just singing for the girls," Aled said, and Gwen's uncle snarled at him.

"You're not paid to sing. Now get on with the milking. I don't want to hear another sound," he shouted, banging the door behind him.

Aled sighed and shook his head.

"I'm sorry," Gwen said, but the labourer smiled.

"It's alright, Gwen. We're all used to your uncle's temper, and you bear it the worst," he replied.

They continued milking in silence, the cows standing patiently above the buckets. When Gwen had filled two, she beckoned Madlen to follow her, the two of them taking the buckets to the dairy, where the milk would be put into churns–some for the milk trains, others to be used for making butter and cheese.

This was a task overseen by Cadell, whose father had put him in charge of the dairy, much to the despair of the labourers who worked there. But as Gwen entered the dairy with Madlen, she was surprised to find no one there. Several muslin bags hung above buckets, dripping the buttermilk for cheese, and pats of butter were waiting to be cut and packed.

None of the labourers were there, even as Gwen heard a sound from the back room, her cousin muttering to himself.

"I've brought the milk, Cadell, where is… oh," Gwen said, entering the back room, where, to her astonishment, she found her cousin bent over one of the churns, pouring what looked like powdered chalk into it.

As she entered, he looked up at her angrily.

"What are you doing here?" he snarled.

"I… I was just bringing the first buckets of milk over. But… what are you doing? What are you putting into the milk?" she asked.

She had never seen anyone putting chalk into milk before, and now the expression on her cousin's face turned to a smirk.

"You're a little fool, aren't you, Gwen? Nothing but a fool. How do you think we send the milk to London?" he asked.

Gwen shook her head. She did not understand. Milk was milk. It came from the cow, it was fresh to drink. She drank a cup of it every day, cold from the dairy, or, in the winter, she warmed it in a pan over the fire and mixed it with honey. She knew her uncle sent large amounts of milk to London–it was the mainstay of their business–but as for what happened to it beforehand…

"In the milk churns," she said, and her cousin rolled his eyes.

"Yes, in the churns, but what do you think we do it with it first?" he replied, with an impatient expression on his face.

"I don't know," Gwen said as Madlen stood silently at her side.

"We put chalk into it. It makes it creamier, it goes further, we make a bigger profit," Cadell replied.

Gwen's eyes grew wide with horror. She had heard of the practice of adulterating milk. Aled had spoken of it. A farm lower down the valley had been closed because of it.

Chalk, or some other noxious substance, had

been added to the milk, just as Cadell was describing. It was illegal to do so, like adding the same to bread in place of flour. Gwen was horrified at what her cousin was doing, even as it seemed her uncle had ordered him to do so.

"But... you can't... it's not right," she stammered, and Cadell rose to his feet, advancing on her, and grabbing her by the wrist.

"Is that so? And what are you going to do about it, Gwen? Do you live under our roof and eat at our table?" he asked, and Gwen nodded.

"I do, but... it's not right to do this, Cadell. People die because of adulterated milk," she said, and Cadell struck her hard across the face, pushing her backwards, as Madlen began to cry.

"And are we supposed to be the ones who die of starvation? Are we to be the ones without a roof over our heads? They won't pay the milk prices; they won't give us a fair price for what we produce. They deserve their adulterated milk," he snarled.

Gwen shook her head. She was horrified, even as she knew her cousin was right. It was a common complaint in the valley–the low price of milk in the cities was driving farmers into poverty, and the farms were becoming unsustainable. But to fill the milk with chalk, to masquerade poison as something to be drunk...

"I… but it's not right, Cadell," she said, and her cousin raised his hand to her a second time.

"And are you going to tell anyone? I only do what my father tells me to do. We put enough chalk in the milk to increase the volume. No one knows. No one's going to die," he said, speaking with his usual misplaced authority, even as there could be no way of telling the effects of the adulterated milk on those who drank it.

The churns were loaded onto the train and sent off to London, replaced by empty ones returned to be filled again. What happened to the milk after it left the valley was a mystery–to Gwen, at least.

"It's wrong," Gwen said, folding her arms and glaring at Cadell, but her cousin only laughed.

"It makes no difference to me. But the back of my hand will to you if you don't get on with the milking. And not a word of this to anyone. That's why I sent the labourers away. No one knows, and no one needs to know. Do you understand me?" he said.

Gwen could do nothing but nod, even as the sheer wickedness of what he and her uncle were doing filled her with loathing. She was trembling as she returned to the milking shed, and Aled looked up at her in surprise.

"You took your time. I've nearly finished," he said, as Gwen sat down at her milking stool.

"I… I was talking to Cadell," she replied, and Aled laughed.

"Or was he just giving you orders? He forgets he's only ten years old. He jumped up a little…" he began, but his words were interrupted by a shout from outside.

"Gwen, where are you?" her uncle called out, and reluctantly, Gwen rose to her feet.

"I'm coming, Uncle Dawid," she called out, and making her way out into the farmyard, she found her uncle pointing up at the meadow.

"Bluebell's due–bring her down to the barn. She'll be calving before the morning," he said.

Gwen looked up to the meadow, where Bluebell was lying down next to the far hedge. Her uncle was right, and it seemed the moment had come.

"Alright, come along, Madlen, let's get Bluebell down to calf," Gwen said, taking her sister's hand in hers.

Ordinarily, she would have been excited at the prospect of a calf being born–especially to Bluebell, her favourite. But as they made their way across the field, Gwen's mind was filled with the horrifying memory of what she had witnessed in the dairy, knowing the wickedness her uncle and cousin were involved in.

"What was Cadell doing to the milk?" Madlen asked as they tried to coax Bluebell to her feet.

"You're too young to understand," Gwen replied, shaking her head.

But Gwen understood all too well, and as they led Bluebell back to the farm, she knew the danger they faced if the adulteration of the milk was discovered–a danger faced by all those who drank it, too.

A DARK SECRET

Gwen watched as the cart loaded with the milk churns made its way down the track from the farm. Aled was leading the horse, and Cadell was sitting on the back shouting orders as several of the labourers walked behind.

Gwen had said nothing to Aled about the adulterated milk, and she had warned her sister to say nothing of what they knew, either. If word got out about the chalk and the farm was closed, Gwen and Madlen would be sent away. The thought of an orphanage or the poorhouse filled her with dread.

She was horrified at what her uncle was doing and having watched the cart disappear down into the valley; she made her way into the barn where her uncle was tending to Bluebell.

"You can sit with her. She's not ready yet, but it's

close. Did the milk cart get away?" her uncle asked, and Gwen nodded.

"We sent two dozen churns," she replied, sitting down in the straw next to heifer and reaching out to stroke her head.

Bluebell lifted her head and let out a low moo. Gwen's uncle rose to his feet, nodding, as he ran his hand over Bluebell's stomach.

"Good, and with plenty of new calves, we should increase the herd this year," he said.

Gwen feared asking the question on her mind, but she knew she had no choice, and as her uncle was leaving, she called out to him.

"Why do you put chalk in the milk, Uncle Dawid?" she asked.

Her uncle turned to her, his face red with anger.

"How do you know that?" he demanded, advancing towards her, and seizing her by the collar.

"I... I saw Cadell doing it. I asked him what he was doing. He told me. I haven't told anyone, I promise. But it's not right, Uncle Dawid, my aunt..." she began, but her uncle cuffed her around the ear.

"Your aunt, what? Wouldn't approve? No, I'm sure she wouldn't. But if I lose the farm, if we all go hungry, if we all end up in the orphanage or poorhouse... what then? Will your morals stretch to stealing a loaf of bread if your stomach's empty, Gwen? Oh, no... you don't know what it's like, do you? You think you can play me for a fool? Well... a little chalk doesn't mean anything. Do you hear me? And if you want to take the moral high ground, I suggest you find somewhere else to live," he snarled.

Gwen looked up at him fearfully, knowing his threats were real. Her lip trembled and tears welled up in her eyes.

"I'm sorry... but... what if someone dies?" she said.

Her uncle let go of her collar and cursed under his breath.

"And if they do, no one will know where the milk came from, only that it came off the milk train from the valleys. There're dozens of farms here. Any one of them could be responsible. But don't judge me, Gwen. Don't judge when you don't know what desperation is," he snarled.

With these words, he turned, marching out of the barn without looking at her again. Madlen appeared at the door and hurried over to Gwen, looking at her expectantly.

"Is Bluebell ready?" she asked.

Gwen looked down at the heifer, whose wide eyes gazed back at her. She stroked the animal's cheek, running her hand over Bluebell's stomach. The time was close, but it would be Bluebell's time, not theirs.

"Nearly, I think. We should stay with her until it

THE MILK MAID ORPHAN

happens," she said, and Madlen sat down in the straw next to her.

"Why did Uncle Dawid look so angry just now?" she asked, and Gwen sighed.

"He misses Aunt Cerian, just like we all do," Gwen replied, and her sister nodded.

"I miss sitting on her lap," she said, and Gwen smiled.

Their aunt would often sit in a rocking chair by the fire in the parlour, and Gwen and Madlen would climb into her lap. She was a wonderful storyteller, and together they would listen to tales of myths and legends told by the light of the fire.

"I do, too," Gwen replied, just as Bluebell let out a snort, mooing loudly.

The time had come, and Gwen now stood up, helping Bluebell roll onto her side. She had seen many calves delivered, and she knew it would be the feet coming first, with a slow and gradual progression every quarter of an hour. The waters had broken, and Gwen sent Madlen to fetch their uncle, stroking Bluebell's face, and whispering words of encouragement.

* * *

It was dark by the time the calf was born, and Gwen had sat with Bluebell for almost three hours, coaxing and reassuring her. Her uncle had come to inspect the heifer, nodding, before returning to the farmhouse, and it was Gwen and Madlen who had been present to witness the act of giving birth. The calf arrived into the world bleating like a lamb, and Gwen helped it to stand, wrapping it in a blanket, as Bluebell watched in some surprise at the offspring she had just delivered.

"Oh, Bluebell, you did so well," Gwen said, smiling at the sight of a new life–of new hope–entering the world.

Madlen patted the calf on the head, stroking it as it staggered around the barn, blinking in the lamplight.

"What do we do now?" she asked.

"We make sure they're both comfortable. The calf needs some milk from its mother," Gwen said, coaxing Bluebell to take an interest in her offspring, as mother and baby now licked one another, and the calf lay down, resting its head on Bluebell's stomach.

Gwen placed a blanket over them both, smiling as the calf looked up at her. She had brought some milk from the dairy–from one of the churns not yet adulterated with chalk–and now she took a spoon and held it to the calf's lips, trying to get it to drink.

"It's drinking, Gwen," Madlen said, and Gwen nodded, taking another spoonful to feed the calf with.

They would have to keep feeding the new-born for the rest of the night – and Bluebell, too. But the hard part was over, the calf was delivered, and mother and baby were doing well.

"Only another dozen or so heifers to birth," Gwen said, smiling at the thought of their repeating this process over again and again in the coming days and weeks.

"Once the first comes, they all come," her aunt used to say, and Gwen had spent many sleepless nights in the barn, helping her aunt and uncle with the calving.

But this year would be different, and Gwen knew her uncle would have little to do with the newborns, even as he would be angry with Gwen if any were lost.

"You go and get some sleep, Madlen. I'll stay with Bluebell," Gwen said, but her sister shook her head.

"I want to stay," she said, sitting down in the straw and stroking Bluebell's head.

They both stayed, taking it in turns to feed the calf, who drank every spoonful of milk given it. It was cold in the barn that night, and as darkness fell that evening, Gwen brought in a lamp from the farmhouse, telling her uncle the calf was proving to be healthy.

"Stay with her for the night," he had told her,

offering no help, even as Cadell had now returned from delivering the churns to the milk train.

Owain was sitting with them, and Gwen's brother did not even look up at her as she collected the lamp from the store cupboard.

"I wish Owain would talk to us," Gwen said as she sat down in the straw next to her sister.

"He's mean to me," Madlen said, and Gwen sighed.

"I fear he's only going to get worse, Madlen," she replied, grateful again to have her sister at her side.

The household was divided, and power lay on the side of Gwen's uncle and cousin. She could do nothing to resist it, even as saw its terrible effects on her brother, whose attitude towards her had completely changed. Would he, too, be taught how to adulterate the milk? It made her shudder to think of it, even as the alternative was worse. If the farm was driven out of business, Gwen and Madlen would be sent to an orphanage, the thought of which did not bear thinking about.

"What will we do?" Madlen asked, and Gwen shook her head.

"We've got one another, Madlen. That's all that matters. And we've got a new friend here, too," Gwen said, looking down at the calf and smiling.

New life meant new hope, and Gwen reached out and placed her hand gently on the calf's forehead. It was warm to the touch, and she stroked it, grateful to have been present at its coming into the world and taking another spoonful of milk to feed it with.

* * *

AFTER BLUEBELL, the calving gathered pace, and half a dozen more calves were born that very week. Gwen and Madlen were kept busy in the barn, sitting with the heifers, coaxing, and encouraging them.

They stayed with the new-borns too, feeding them, and making sure the mothers accepted their new offspring. Some of the births were more complicated than others, and one of the calves died after having been turned in the womb and suffocated.

Madlen had cried, but Gwen had explained there could be no sentimentality over such things–her aunt had taught her that much.

"Nature doesn't always behave as we might wish it to, Madlen. It's not unusual for calves to die–their mothers, too. It's a dangerous business giving birth, and you and I don't have the expertise to help as we might wish," Gwen had said.

Had her aunt been there, she might have saved the unborn calf. Gwen had often watched her aunt assisting the calving–hauling calves out of their mothers with her own hands.

Gwen and Madlen could only do their best. When all the heifers had given birth, the herd had several dozen new members, replacing those sent for slaughter. Gwen was kept busy, back, and forth between the barn and the milking shed.

"You did well," Aled told her, even as Gwen had received no word of thanks from her uncle, who spent all his time in the dairy with Cadell and Owain.

"I'm glad we only lost one. I was worried there would be more stillborns," Gwen said, but Aled shook his head.

"You were there with every one, Gwen. You *and* Madlen. It makes a difference when they're not on their own. I'm sure your uncle's grateful," he said, and Gwen sighed.

"I doubt it. He was angry with me for losing one. He blamed me for it," she said.

Her uncle had flown into a rage when she had told him about the dead calf. He had told her it was her fault, and that she should have been concentrating better on the task at hand. Gwen had tried to explain, even as she had known there was nothing more she could have done for the heifer, or her calf.

"He blames anyone but himself. He's a changed man. My mother says I should look elsewhere for a job. She worries about me working here. There're rumours. Not that I want to speak ill of your uncle, though I don't mind doing so about your cousin– and I know you feel the same," Aled said, shaking his head.

Gwen was curious. She had not said anything to anyone about the adulterated milk, knowing it was a secret she could not afford to reveal.

"What sort of rumours?" she asked.

Aled glanced at the milk shed door, leaning forward, and lowering his voice.

"My mother says they're adulterating the milk– adding chalk to it. Your uncle was seen at the quarry over in Isgoed. He was buying chalk," Aled said.

Gwen tried to appear surprised, even as Aled's story fitted the facts she already knew to be true.

"Chalk? In the milk, you mean?" she said, and Aled nodded.

"That's right. They'll put just enough to make it look creamy and thicken it. Some do the opposite. They water it down. But your uncle's chosen to make it thick. He'll be selling it to the upmarket London hotels, calling it cream," he said, shaking his head.

"But that can't be right. What… what would happen if he was discovered to be doing it?" Gwen asked.

She feared to know the answer, even as Aled looked grave.

"It's illegal, Gwen. He'll go to prison, and they'll close the farm down. If someone dies because of it, he'll hang–if they can trace it back to the farm for certain. The churns have numbers on them. They put them on when they're loaded onto the trains. My Godfather's a guard at the station, he says so," Aled said.

Gwen's heart skipped a beat. Her uncle had claimed the milk could not be traced. But if the churns were numbered, and if someone fell ill and died from drinking the milk from one... it made her shudder to think of it, and she shook her head, sickened by what her uncle and cousin were doing.

"And you're certain they're doing this?" she asked.

"I know they are. I've seen the chalk. They think I don't know. But it's in the wood store, hidden behind the logs. Bags of it. It's your cousin who puts it in. He sends the labourers away from the dairy, then takes the churns into the back where they make the cheese. He uses a whole sack of chalk. It's too much. Lots of people do it, I know. But people are dying because of it. It's only a matter of time before someone dies because of your uncle and cousin. My mother says I should leave, but you don't have the choice of that, Gwen. I wanted to warn you. But don't say a word of it to your uncle. Do you understand me?" he said, and Gwen nodded.

She already knew the terrible truth, and now she feared she could be classed as a colluder in this wicked scheme, should someone meet their death after drinking the adulterated milk.

"I do, but... I don't know what to do. I can't confront my uncle. He'd know you'd told me. And as for my cousin..." she said, her words trailing off at the thought of the look Cadell had given her when she had discovered what he was doing.

"I'm worried about Owain, Gwen. They'll have him doing the same. And the magistrate won't care whose neck goes in the noose – if someone's punished for it," Aled said.

Gwen was worried, too. She knew her brother was entirely under the influence of her cousin and uncle. He had a slyness about him, and was forever spying on Gwen and Madlen, ready to report the smallest of misdemeanours.

"You should find a new job, Aled. You can't be mixed up in all of this," Gwen said, but the labourer shook his head.

"I already am, Gwen. It's a sorry truth," he replied, shaking his head, before leaving the milking shed.

Gwen sighed. She was fearful for the future, not knowing what would become of her and Madlen should the truth be revealed, and her uncle and cousin arrested. They would be taken to the poorhouse or the orphanage. It made her shudder to think about it, and she sighed, brushing a tear from her eye.

"If only Aunt Cerian was still here," she said to herself, knowing her aunt would not have stood for such wickedness. And with a heavy heart, she went to check on Bluebell and her calf, the work of the farm unceasing.

A SURPRISING SONG

Whenever she could, Gwen would slip away from the farm, walking on the hilltops surrounding it, or down into the valley below. She liked to be alone with her own thoughts, even as Madlen often insisted on following her.

She was like a puppy following its master, and with lambing season now under way, she had acquired several charges of her own. Lambs following her wherever she went.

"Why don't you stay here and play with your lambs, Madlen?" Gwen said.

It was a Saturday afternoon and all the jobs on the farm had been seen to–the calving season was over, and the herd was grazing happily in the meadow behind the barn.

The milking had been done, and Gwen's uncle and cousin, along with her brother, had taken the horse and cart to the village. Only Aled remained at the farm, and he was snoozing in the henhouse, where Gwen had just been to collect eggs.

"Can't I come with you?" Madlen asked, but Gwen shook her head.

"I want to be on my own, Madlen," she said, and Madlen looked up at her with wide, tearful eyes.

"What if you don't come back?" she asked, her lips trembling.

Gwen smiled and put her arms around her sister.

"I'm going to walk to the chapel and visit Aunt Cerian. You can come next time. Besides, someone needs to stay here and look after the animals. You'll have Branwen," Gwen said, and at the sound of his name, the oldest of the sheepdogs came lumbering out of the farmhouse.

Gwen knew her sister would be safe at the farm for a few hours. Aled was there, and Branwen was a loyal and trusted companion. Madlen nodded, though she looked miserable at being left out. Calling for her three lambs to follow her, she made her way back inside.

Gwen was glad to be on her own, and she made her way across the farmyard and out of the gate into the lane leading down to the valley. Everywhere was lush and green, a gentle breeze was blowing, and the sky was blue, with wisps of white cloud high above.

The sound of bleating lambs echoed over the hillsides, and Gwen found herself smiling at the sight of the abundant new life all around her. But the idyllic scene masked a sinister underbelly, and Gwen could not help but think of the wickedness her uncle and cousin were involved with.

Every day, churns of milks were sent down from the farm to the railway station, and every day, in the far-off metropolis, unwitting victims were drinking the milk adulterated with chalk in the dairy. It made Gwen shudder to think of it.

"And how soon before someone dies?" she asked herself, for she had heard rumours of inspections and the discovery of other farms in other valleys doing just the same.

The consequences were unthinkable, even as it seemed her uncle had no regard for the dangers involved. The milk continued to be adulterated, and there seemed to be no prick of conscience when it came to the thought of what he was doing.

Cadell, too, was without a moral compass, and it was he who added the chalk each day, making the milk appear thick and creamy…

"But it can't continue. They won't get away with it, not forever," Gwen thought to herself.

She had the horrible feeling she herself was responsible, too. She knew what was happening, and yet to say anything, to report anything, would have meant the certainty of the poorhouse or orphanage, and the wrath of her uncle and cousin.

Like Aled, Gwen had chosen silence, even as she knew it was wrong to do so. But now she tried to dismiss such thoughts, glancing back up the hill towards the farm, before setting her sights on the path ahead.

She was making her way to the chapel, and she paused to pick wildflowers from a bank off the path, intending to lay a posy on her aunt's grave. Gwen often visited the chapel graveyard.

She liked to sit with her aunt, imagining her as she had once known her, with her rosy cheeks and smile. Gwen would tell her things, or sometimes simply sit in silence with tears rolling down her cheeks. She missed her aunt terribly, and she knew her death had brought about the wickedness her uncle now took for granted.

Adulterating the milk was a way of life. It was for profit and greed and Gwen knew her aunt would never have agreed to it.

"We have the best milk, from the best herd in all of Wales," she used to say, smiling proudly at the sight of the new-borns in the field.

When Gwen reached the chapel, she found the graveyard deserted, and approaching her aunt's grave, she kneeled in front of it. The stone was simple, made of slate with a plain inscription, already weathering, detailed her aunt's name and dates. Gwen placed the posy of flowers in front of it, reaching out to touch the stone, tracing her fingers along the curve.

It felt rough to the touch, hewed from the stone of the surrounding hills, just like the chapel itself. A blackbird was singing in a tree above, and Gwen looked up, smiling, as the bird flew down and hopped forward, pulling a worm up from the ground.

"I wish I could fly away," she said, and the bird cocked its head, looking at her as if to say, "why can't you?"

It hopped around for a few moments more, pulling up another worm, before flying back up to the tree above. Gwen looked back at her aunt's grave, sighing, as she wondered what her aunt would say at the thought of the burden she was bearing. She would surely be horrified, not only to think of the milk being adulterated, but of how Gwen's uncle had involved not only Cadell, but Owain, too.

"But I don't know what to do. Who can I tell?" she said, feeling helpless.

The blackbird was singing in the tree above, and the gentle breeze was blowing across the graveyard. Gwen sighed, knowing there would be no answer. But as she rose to her feet, she was surprised by the sound of another song, a voice echoing on the breeze.

"Down by the sea, red roses are blooming;
Down by the sea, white lilies are gleaming;
Down by the sea, my true love is dwelling,
Sleeping all night, rising up in the morning.

Down where the sea laps at the flat rock
My love and I did wander and talk;
All around us grew the white lily,
And there were sprigs of rosemary.

IT WAS BEAUTIFUL, and rising to her feet, Gwen looked around her for the source of the voice. It was a boy, perhaps a few years older than she, sitting on the steps of the chapel. He had tousled blonde hair and a fair face, his hands clasped together as he sang. He was wearing the simple clothes of a labourer, and

Gwen could only assume he lived on one of the farms in the valley.

> "By the seaside are blue stones
> By the seaside are the sons' flowers
> By the seaside is every virtue
> By the seaside is my sweetheart.
>
> Full the sea of sand and billows
> Full the egg of whites and yellows
> Full the woods of leaf and flower
> Full my heart of love forever."

GWEN APPROACHED THE BOY, enchanted by the sound of his voice. He looked up at her and smiled. There was no embarrassment in his expression, and Gwen smiled back at him, wanting only to hear the conclusion of the song.

"Please, don't stop for me," she said, as the boy rose to his feet.

"Did you like it? It's just an old song my grandmother taught me," he said, and Gwen nodded.

"I liked it a lot. But how does it end?" she asked.

"Oh, there's just one more verse," he said, and Gwen smiled.

"Will you sing it for me?" she asked, and the boy nodded, still standing on the chapel steps as he took a deep breath, his voice ringing out clear and sweet.

> "Fair the sun at new day's dawning
> Fair the rainbow's colour shining
> Fair the summer, fair as heaven
> Fairer yet, the face of Elin."

"THAT WAS BEAUTIFUL. But who was Elin?" Gwen said, entirely taken up by the story told in the song and captivated by thoughts of the seashore and the dawn breaking over the waters.

"I don't know–it's just a song," the boy said, grinning at Gwen, who laughed.

"But where did you learn it? Where did you learn to sing so beautifully?" she asked, for she had never heard anyone sing as the boy had sung.

The Welsh valleys were famous for their choirs, but that of the Talfryn chapel had long since fallen by the wayside. A few of the older men still sang occasionally but gone were the days of a thirty strong choir, resounding the praises of God through song.

"I've always loved to sing. My grandmother teaches me the words. She remembers the old songs, but she can't sing them. She hums the tunes and tells me the words. I love to sing," he said.

Gwen had never seen the boy before, though it seemed he was familiar with the valley, and the chapel. She liked him. He had an ease of manner about him, and his smile lit up his face.

"So, you know others, too?" she asked, and the boy nodded.

"I know lots of songs. I sing all day," he said, jumping down the chapel steps to stand in front of her.

Gwen knew only a handful of songs. Her aunt had often sung to her, but the words were forgotten and confused. Gwen tried to remember one, not wanting the boy to think she knew nothing of the great tradition the valleys were so famous for.

"Do you know Myfanwy?" Gwen asked, for it was the only one she could remember.

The boy nodded.

"Why so the anger, oh Myfanwy
That fill your dark eyes

> Your gentle cheeks, oh Myfanwy
> No longer blush beholding me?
> Where now the smile upon your lips
> That lit my foolish faithful love?
> Where now the sound of your sweet words,
> That drew my heart to follow you?"

GWEN TRIED her best to join in, but the boy sang too quickly, and his voice was so pure and sweet as to drown out Gwen's own, less than tuneful, attempts. But the song was one she remembered her aunt singing to her when she was very small, and the words–and hearing them sung–brought back many happy memories.

"You're very clever," Gwen said, but the boy only shook his head and laughed.

"I just listen and repeat the words," he said, shrugging his shoulders.

Gwen smiled at him.

"I'm Gwen," she said, realising he had sung to her, but neither of them knew the other's name.

"I'm Bryn, Bryn Kneath," he said, smiling back at her.

Gwen had heard the name of Kneath before. There were Kneaths at the far end of the valley, but she had never heard of a Bryn Kneath before.

"Gwen Parry. I live at Talfryn Farm with my uncle and cousin, and my sister and brother, too," Gwen said, glancing back up the valley to where the farm could just be made out on the hillside above.

Bryn nodded.

"Your aunt died, didn't she? My grandmother said she was a good and gentle woman," he said.

It made Gwen happy to hear her aunt so described, even as Bryn's words were tinged with the sadness of her loss. She nodded.

"She was. And you live with your grandmother?" she asked.

The boy nodded.

"That's right. My father was a shepherd. He died before I was born out on the hill in the winter, and my mother was a milkmaid, but she died in childbirth. I've always lived with my grandmother. I don't know any other life," he said.

Gwen could sympathise with him. They had both lost their parents, raised by others, never to know what their lives might have been like otherwise.

"Neither do I. I came to Talfryn Farm after my sister was born. Our mother died in childbirth, too. We've lived there ever since," Gwen said.

Bryn nodded, glancing up to the chapel door. It was as though he was waiting for something, and Gwen wondered what had brought him to the chapel on that sunny afternoon.

"Did you come to visit your aunt?" he asked, and Gwen nodded.

"I often come. I like to be close to her," she said.

"I'm waiting for Reverend Llewelyn. He's trying to get the choir going again, and my grandmother told him I could sing. He said to come and sing for him, so here I am. But he's late, I think," he said.

But at these words, the familiar figure of the minister appeared at the gate into the graveyard, and he smiled at them, nodding as he approached.

"I'm sorry, Bryn, I got caught up talking to Mrs. Maddocks on my way, once she starts…" he said, taking out a key from his pocket.

He did not question Gwen's presence but led them both into the chapel. It felt strange to be there without the hustle and bustle of a crowd around them, and Gwen sat down on one of the pews, looking up at the plain wooden cross behind the small table at the back.

"Will I be able to sing, Reverend Llewelyn? In the choir, I mean," Bryn said, and the minister nodded.

"If your grandmother's to be believed, yes, Bryn. But I want to hear you for myself. I see you've got an audience," he said, glancing at Gwen, who blushed.

"May I stay?" she asked, and Bryn grinned at her.

"You've already heard me sing. You can hear me again," he said, and Reverend Llewelyn nodded.

"You can stay, Gwen. I'll play something on the

organ, Bryn. Take one of the hymn books—I want to hear you sing out nice and clear," Reverend Llewelyn said, taking a seat on the organ stool.

He started off the pump, the organ breathing into life, and now he played an introduction, the instrument thundering around the chapel.

"Love divine, all loves excelling,
joy of heav'n to earth come down,
fix in us Thy humble dwelling;
all Thy faithful mercies crown!
Jesus, Thou art all compassion,
pure, unbounded love Thou art;
visit us with Thy salvation;
enter every trembling heart.

Breathe, O breathe Thy loving Spirit
into every troubled breast!
Let us all in Thee inherit,
let us find the promised rest.
Take away our love of sinning;
Alpha and Omega be;
end of faith, as its beginning,
set our hearts at liberty."

. . .

BRYN'S VOICE rang out clearly around the chapel, and once again, Gwen was captivated by his performance. He sang with such passion and conviction, and with a voice far beyond his years. Reverend Llewelyn, too, seemed impressed, and he nodded, turning from the organ and smiling.

"Very good, Bryn. You've got a remarkable voice. Your grandmother was right, and I'm glad to have heard you for myself. You'll be a fine addition to our new choir," the minister said, and Bryn clapped his hands together in delight.

"Do you really mean it, Reverend Llewelyn?" he asked, and the minister nodded.

"Absolutely, Bryn. We're holding our first rehearsal this Friday evening. Be here for six O'clock, and you can meet the others. We'll just sing through the Sunday morning hymns at first. But I hope to develop the choir into something more as the months go on–a concert at Christmas, perhaps, or a celebration for the harvest," he said.

Gwen was pleased for Bryn. He had a beautiful voice, and the choir would be all the better for having him as part of it. A sudden thought now occurred to her, and summoning her courage, she approached Reverend Llewelyn, who was examining the stops on the organ and muttering to himself.

"Excuse me, Reverend Llewelyn. Might I be able to join the choir?" Gwen asked.

The thought of doing so was exciting. In her day-to-day life, Gwen had little to look forward to. She saw to her jobs around the farm, and to her duties in the house. She liked to sing, even as she did not know whether she was any good at it or not. The minister looked at her and smiled.

"Well… it's usually only men and boys who sing in the valley choirs. But if you *can* sing," he said, returning his attentions to the organ.

He struck up the same tune again, indicating for Bryn to show Gwen the hymnbook from which he had been singing.

> "Come, Almighty, to deliver;
> let us all Thy life receive;
> suddenly return and never,
> nevermore Thy temples leave.
> Thee we would be always blessing,
> serve Thee as Thy hosts above;
> pray, and praise Thee without ceasing,
> glory in Thy perfect love.

> Finish then, Thy new creation;

pure and spotless, let us be;
let us see Thy great salvation
perfectly restored in Thee.
Changed from glory into glory,
till in heav'n we take our place,
till we cast our crowns before Thee,
lost in wonder, love, and praise."

Gwen's own attempt at the hymn, one she knew well enough from having sang it in the chapel, was lacklustre at best, and as the music came to an end, Reverend Llewelyn turned to her and raised his eyebrows.

"A little more practice, perhaps, Gwen," he said.

Gwen felt disappointed, even as Bryn smiled at her.

"You did well," he said, as Gwen closed the book with a sigh.

"But I can't be in the choir?" she asked.

The minister looked at her sympathetically.

"Well… not immediately. But a little practice," he said, glancing at Bryn, who nodded.

"I'll help you. We can sing together. You just need to practice," he said, and Gwen smiled.

She was grateful to him, and as they left the

chapel that afternoon, Bryn promised to teach Gwen how to sing.

"Come to the farm. We can practice in one of the barns," Gwen said, as they parted ways outside the chapel gate, and as she returned to the farm that afternoon, it was with a renewed sense of hope that something better was to come.

SINGING LESSONS

In the days that followed, Gwen thought of little else but her encounter with Bryn at the chapel, and the prospect of him teaching her to sing. It excited her, and as she milked the cows and went about her jobs and duties, she hummed to herself, taking care of how the words she sang might sound, and how she could improve her rehearsal.

"And the stars came out, and they dwelt at night, and they shone 'til the early morn," she sang to herself, humming the last few notes as she milked Bluebell in the milking shed.

"What's that you're singing?" a voice behind her asked, and looking up, she found Aled standing behind her.

Gwen blushed. She had not thought anyone was listening.

"Oh… it's just a song about the stars. Aunt Cerian used to sing it to me," Gwen replied.

"You're not thinking of joining Reverend Llewelyn's choir, are you?" Aled asked.

Gwen nodded. There had been much talk in the valley about the revival of the chapel choir, and several of the labourers had tried out for an audition–Aled included.

"I heard one of the auditions the other day. A boy called Bryn. He was very good," Gwen said, not wanting to tell Aled of her own ambitions.

The labourer looked at her and smiled.

"Reverend Llewelyn said my voice was too deep. Too deep? We're in the valley. What does he expect?" he asked, shaking his head.

"Maybe you could try again–you could sing something else?" Gwen said, for she knew how much Aled liked to sing.

He was always singing something, as were many of the other labourers on the farm. There was a saying in Talfryn Valley– "the hills are a song"–and if it was not the sound of sheep or cattle on the air, it was the sound of a fair voice and a fair song.

"I don't know, perhaps. But is this your friend coming now?" Aled said, pointing out of the milking shed door to the gate leading into the farmyard.

Gwen looked out, and to her delight, she saw Bryn, carrying several books under his arm.

Hastily, she finished milking Bluebell before hurrying out to greet him. He looked at her and smiled.

"I hope I haven't come at a bad time," he said, but Gwen shook her head.

She did not care what her uncle or cousin might say, even as she knew they would not approve of her learning to sing or making a new friend.

"Not at all. We can go into one of the barns," Gwen said, beckoning him to follow her.

Madlen now appeared from the henhouse, looking at Gwen inquisitively.

"Who's that?" she asked, pointing at Bryn, who smiled.

"This is Bryn, Madlen, and don't point, it's rude," Gwen said.

Madlen followed them towards the barn behind the milking shed. It was used to store grain and other food for the animals, but in the summer, it went largely unused, and Gwen hoped they would not be disturbed.

"Are you ready to sing?" Bryn asked, and Gwen nodded.

She felt suddenly nervous, even as she had been singing all morning in the milking shed. But Bryn was possessed of such a talent as to make her own attempts seem feeble in place of it. He had brought a hymn book from the chapel, though Gwen had another reason to be embarrassed at the thought of singing in front of him.

"I don't know how to read, not properly," she said, and he looked at her in surprise.

"But you sang the hymn the other day," he said.

"Because I recognised the tune," she replied.

She expected him to be angry, but he only smiled and nodded.

"It's alright. I'll start you off. Do you know some of the more famous ones?" he asked, and Gwen nodded.

She knew lots of songs by heart, but not from having read them. She had a keen ear, and any song her aunt had sung to her, she could repeat word for word.

"You start one, then I can join in," she said, and Bryn opened the hymn book, flicking through the pages, before tapping his finger on the spine and smiling.

"Guide me, O my great Redeemer,
pilgrim through this barren land;
I am weak, but you are mighty;
hold me with your powerful hand.
Bread of heaven, bread of heaven,
feed me now and evermore,
feed me now and evermore."

. . .

THE HYMN WAS one of the most familiar to Gwen, and she even had a vague memory of her father singing it when she was a child. She knew the words by heart, and Bryn had stopped singing, allowing her to continue solo. As she concluded, he smiled and nodded, clapping his hands as she looked at him for approval.

"You've got a beautiful voice, Gwen. It's just a little… low. You need to raise it up. Imagine you're singing to the whole valley. Picture yourself standing on Mervgyn's Rock," he said, and Gwen smiled.

Mervgyn's Rock lay at the end of a path through the woods above the chapel. It was a large boulder, and the intrepid could climb to the top and look out over the whole valley. There was a legend of a knight, Sir Mervgyn, singing to his lover from the rock, the song echoing through the valley and awakening her from a hundred-year slumber.

"But I don't want to shout," Gwen said, and Bryn shook his head.

"There's a difference between shouting and singing so others can hear you. Your voice needs to resound. Let's try the next verse. Do you know it?" he said, and Gwen nodded.

> "Open now, the crystal fountain,
> where the healing waters flow.
> Let the fire and cloudy pillar
> lead me all my journey through.
> Strong Deliverer, strong Deliverer,
> ever be my strength and shield,
> ever be my strength and shield."

BRYN LISTENED AS SHE SANG, and even Madlen, who had appeared bored before, sat listening, holding one of her pet lambs in her arms. This time, Gwen sang clearly, trying to raise her voice, though being careful not to shout. The words of the hymn echoed around the barn, and Bryn nodded approvingly.

"Excellent, yes. That's just what I meant. You sound so much better, Gwen," he said, and Gwen smiled.

She hoped he was not just being kind, even as she knew she would never match Bryn's own abilities when it came to song.

"Do you really mean it?" she asked, and he nodded.

"I wouldn't say so if I didn't. You've got a fine voice. You just need to keep practicing. Let's sing the final verse together," he said, clearing his throat.

> "When I tread the verge of Jordan,
> bid my anxious fears subside.
> Death of death, and hell's Destruction,
> land me safe on Canaan's side.
> Songs of praises, songs of praises
> I will ever sing to you,
> I will ever sing to you."

THE FINAL WORDS resounded around the barn, and Gwen and Bryn smiled at one another, caught up in the pleasure of the words, of the tune, and of the song. But as the last notes resounded, Gwen heard footsteps outside the barn, and an angry voice now called out.

"What's all this?" Gwen's uncle said, striding into the barn and glaring angrily at Gwen and Bryn.

"Gwen was singing," Madlen said, and their uncle snarled at her.

"Singing? And what's singing got to do with working?" he demanded.

Bryn looked nervous, but Gwen was not about to be forbidden from the one thing she found to bring her pleasure.

"Bryn was helping me practice for the choir, Uncle. Lots of the labourers are taking part. The whole valley's talking about it," she said.

Her uncle narrowed his eyes, glaring at Bryn, who nodded.

"It's true, they are, sir. Reverend Llewelyn wants to revive the tradition of a valley choir. Gwen's got a beautiful voice. She just needs some practice, that's all," he said.

"Practice? She needs some practice at her work and her duties," her uncle said, looking angrily at Gwen, who felt tears rising in her eyes.

Her uncle was being needlessly cruel. There was no reason to forbid her from singing or chastise her for doing so.

"Why shouldn't I sing? Aunt Cerian always sung. She had a beautiful voice. Don't you remember?" she asked.

At the mention of her aunt, Gwen's uncle turned his face away. He never mentioned her, and this was the first time Gwen had done so in his presence for many months.

"Your aunt… sing in your own time, Gwen," he said, before marching out of the barn and slamming the door behind him.

Gwen was trembling with anger, even as Bryn began to apologise.

"I'm sorry, I didn't realise…" he said, but Gwen shook her head.

"It's alright. He… he gets angry," she said, sitting down on a bale of hay and sighing.

Madlen came over to her, leading her pet lamb by a piece of rope around its neck. She put her head on Gwen's knee and looked up at her.

"You sang nicely, Gwen," she said, and Gwen smiled, stroking her sister's head.

Bryn sat down next to them.

"You did. You should keep practicing. We don't have to do it here. We could meet in the valley somewhere, maybe even at Mervgyn's Rock?" he said.

Gwen smiled. She was grateful to him for his kindness. They hardly knew one another, but a love of singing had brought them together, and Gwen was only too happy to think their rehearsals might continue.

"Do you think I'll ever be good enough for the choir?" she asked, and he nodded.

"Absolutely. We all need to practice, and it'll take time before we can sing like a real Welsh choir," he said, opening the hymn book and humming another tune.

It was one Gwen recognised.

"Love divine, all loves excelling,
joy of heav'n, to earth come down,
fix in us thy humble dwelling,
all thy faithful mercies crown.
Jesus, thou art all compassion,

> pure, unbounded love thou art.
> Visit us with thy salvation;
> enter ev'ry trembling heart."

THEY SANG IT TOGETHER, though keeping their voices low for fear of rousing Gwen's uncle's wrath yet again. Madlen sat listening, stroking her pet lamb's back, and smiling. When they had finished the verse, she clapped.

"Another one," she said, but Gwen shook her head.

"I think that's enough for today," she said, and Bryn nodded.

"I need to get back to my grandmother. She'll worry about me otherwise," he said.

Gwen was curious to know what Bryn's grandmother was like. She pictured an ancient figure, bent over, or sitting in a rocking chair, but with a smile like that of her aunt.

"Is she very old?" she asked, and Bryn smiled.

"As old as the hills, that's how old she says she feels, at least," he replied.

They made their way out of the barn into the sunshine. Madlen followed with her lamb, and Gwen walked with Bryn to the farmyard gate, glad to have had his company, even as she felt sorry for her uncle's behaviour.

"You will come back, won't you?" she asked, and Bryn nodded.

"I will. But next time, we should meet at Mervgyn's Rock," he said, and Gwen agreed.

She watched him go, standing with Madlen at the farm gate, glad to have made a new and unexpected friend.

"I like him," Madlen said, and Gwen smiled.

"I like him, too," she replied.

* * *

IN THE COMING DAYS, Gwen continued to practice her singing, though she was careful to do so only when her uncle was out of earshot. He did not approve of the choir, telling her the minister should do more praying and less singing, but there was much enthusiasm in the valley for the choir, and all the labourers on the farm had been auditioned.

Gwen was grateful to her aunt for all the songs she had taught her, from the great chapel hymns to the simple ballads of the countryside. She knew dozens of tunes and would even make up her own songs as she was milking the cows.

"I'm going to make a song up about you, Bluebell," Gwen said as she sat on the milking stool with the cow standing patiently in front of her.

Bluebell tossed her head nonchalantly. Her calf was at her side, sitting in the straw, and as Gwen began to milk her, she tried rhyming different words into a song.

"Bluebell... the milker... the meadows... if I should come to the hill country, where milkers roam so freely," she sang, though the tune was proving elusive, and shaking her head, she concentrated on her milking.

But footsteps behind her caused her to look up, and she was surprised to find her brother watching her from the milking shed door. Owain rarely spoke to her, except to demand something. He was just five years old, nearly six, but already he had the slyness and cunning of one far beyond his years. Gwen did not like the way he looked at her, and she raised her eyebrows, waiting for him to speak.

"Cadell says to hurry up and bring the milk," he said.

Gwen glared at him. He was always telling her and Madlen what to do. Their uncle treated him as a second son. Owain sat at the table to eat and had a chair by the fire. He was being taught to view himself as superior to his sisters and was never tasked with menial chores or errands. Owain was Cadell's pet, and where Cadell went, Owain followed.

"I've not finished yet," Gwen replied.

"Then get a move on," Owain said.

"And what's the hurry? Why don't you help? You're old enough to milk a cow," Gwen retorted.

Owain advanced on her, holding up his hand as though to strike her. She moved out of the way, raising her hands to defend herself. Owain kicked over the bucket, sending Bluebell's milk spilling over the flagstone floor.

"You do as you're told," Owain said, reaching out and pinching Gwen hard on the arm.

She let out a cry, but as she did so, Bluebell turned, snorting angrily. Perhaps she thought her calf was in danger, or perhaps Gwen's kindness over the years had brought about a genuine affection on Bluebell's part. Either way, the animal now lashed out, kicking at Owain, and butting him so hard he fell back with a cry, sprawling on the floor as Gwen picked herself up.

"There, now, you deserved that, Owain," Gwen said, as her brother started to cry.

But Gwen had no sympathy for him. He had made his bed, and now he could lie in it. He was whimpering, holding his leg, and Bluebell now turned to Gwen, nuzzling her nose into her as Gwen stroked the cows' ears.

"You'll be sorry," Owain said, but Gwen shook her head.

THE MILK MAID ORPHAN

"I already am. Sorry at the thought of what a nasty little creature you've become. Run off back to Cadell. Tell him he'll have his milk when the cows are ready," she said.

Owain, limping on his right leg, went off muttering to himself, and Gwen returned to her milking, smiling at Bluebell, who now adopted her usual placid demeanour. When the milking was finished, Gwen took the first of the churns across to the dairy.

She knew Owain would have told Cadell about what had happened in the milking shed, and no doubt her uncle would be angry with her later, too. But as she entered the dairy, Gwen could hear low voices coming from the backroom, and pausing, she listened.

"You need to learn how this is done, Owain. You watch your cousin, now. A little chalk, not too much, and stir it in. That's it, good boy. Keep pouring it in… and stop. Now stir. Do you see how it thickens the milk? That's just what we want it to do," Cadell was saying.

Gwen set down the churn quietly, approaching the door at the back of the dairy and peering into the room behind. Cadell and Owain were bent over one of the churns, and a large sack of powdered chalk stood at their side. It was obvious what they were doing, and the thought of it made Gwen's blood run cold.

"What happens if you put too much in?" Owain asked.

"Too much isn't good for anyone. It's an art to put in just the right amount. Too much and it can be poisonous. But a little makes the milk creamy, and that's what those who drink it want. A little more now," Cadell said, and Owain took a handful of chalk from the bag, dropping it into the churn and mixing it in with a large stick.

Cadell nodded with satisfaction, and Gwen cleared her throat, causing the two to look up in surprise.

"She's spying on us," Owain said, rising angrily to his feet.

Gwen looked at him with disdain.

"I know what you're doing," she said, as her cousin rose to his feet.

He smirked at her.

"And I suppose we're to receive another moralising from you, Gwen," he said, folding his arms.

But Gwen shook her head.

"You it's wrong. I don't need to tell you it's wrong. And involving Owain in it, too… it's wicked," she said, but her cousin only shrugged.

"He's got to learn one day. He'll be doing it himself soon enough. Now keep quiet, and bring the other churns in. Or would you prefer the alternative, Gwen? It's this, or the poorhouse, or the orphanage– it's your choice. Don't judge us when you're benefiting from it, too," he said, still smirking at her.

Gwen knew he was right, and she felt a terrible sense of guilt for her involvement, even as she hated the thought of what they were doing.

"I... I don't want anything to do with it," she said, and her cousin laughed.

"Then turn your face away, Gwen. But if hear another word of judgement from you..." he said, allowing his threat to linger in the air.

Gwen retreated from the dairy, hurrying back out into the farmyard as tears rolled down her cheeks. She was trapped, caught up in the terrible secret she could not escape from.

Owain would only become more involved, and she knew she had lost her brother, even as she wanted desperately to protect her sister. For Madlen's sake, she would keep the secret, but it was a terrible burden to bear.

She left the milk in the milking shed, wanting nothing more to do with the farm that day, and hurried off down the lane, making in the direction of Mervgyn's Rock. She was due to meet Bryn there that day, and for several hours, she sat waiting on top of the enormous boulder, reached by a fallen tree perched against it to create a walkway.

Looking out over the valley, Gwen wept bitterly, mourning the loss of her aunt, and the sad fate she could look forward to if the truth about the adulterated milk was revealed. It was terrible, and she felt powerless as to what she could do…

"Are you alright?" a voice behind her asked, and looking up, she found Bryn standing on the log, looking down at her.

She pulled out a handkerchief and dried her eyes, feeling embarrassed at having been caught amid her tears.

"Oh… I'm sorry, it's just…" she said, and then it all came out.

She told Bryn about the milk, how it was adulterated, and how her cousin was leading her brother into wicked ways. She told Bryn of the ways her uncle treated them, sobbing as she recounted how happy she had once been before the untimely death of her aunt.

Bryn listened, sitting next to her on the top of Mervgyn's Rock. He remained quiet, allowing her to talk, his comforting presence giving her the strength to continue, knowing she had to confide in someone lest the unthinkable should happen.

"They're not the only ones doing it, adulterating the milk, I mean. It's happening all over the valley, in every valley. That's what my grandmother says," he said, and Gwen nodded.

"I've heard the same. It's terrible," she said, shaking her head.

"I'm sorry," Bryn said, and Gwen smiled weakly, wiping the tears from her eyes.

"I'm just glad I've told someone," she said, and Bryn smiled back at her.

"Well, shall we sing? Whenever I've got a problem, I find singing it out really helps," he said, and Gwen nodded.

She was glad to do so, glad to have a song to sing, even as hope seemed in short supply, and as Bryn hummed a tune, the two of them sang out across the valley, their voices echoing around the hills–a song to cheer their hearts and give hope to better times ahead.

PART II

AS OLD AS THE HILLS

Wales, Winter, 1860

Gwen was now twelve years old, and life in the valley had continued in much the same way for the past five years. Each day, Gwen would rise early, before dawn, to milk the cows, leading them from the barn into the milking shed.

Her sister was old enough to help her now, and the two of them would talk, or sing, as they milked, encouraging the cows to yield. During calving season, they were kept busy in the barn and meadow, and it was the same with the lambs, too. The rhythms of the years, agricultural and religious, were their markers, and it was a way of life with little change or alteration, even as Gwen remained fearful as to how easily it could be taken away.

Her uncle and cousin, assisted by her brother,

still adulterated the milk each day, mixing it with chalk, before sending it down the valley to where the steam train would take it to London. It was second nature now, as though it *was* normal to poison milk with chalk in pursuit of profit.

"You won't stop them," Bryn said, as Gwen walked with him to the chapel.

After much practice, and a little persuasion on Bryn's part, Reverend Llewelyn had been persuaded to allow Gwen to join the choir. It had grown from a few talented labourers to a full voice choir, known beyond the valley for its songs, both sacred and secular.

They met each week at the chapel on a Friday evening to practice, before singing as part of the service on Sunday. It was Gwen's favourite time of the week, and she would wait for Bryn at the bottom of the track leading up to the farm, the two of them walking to the chapel together.

"I know I won't. There's only one thing that's ever going to stop them, and that's being caught. But there's never been an inspection of the farm, and no one would know the milk was being adulterated. I've heard Cadell telling Owain often enough how they do it, just enough to make it creamy, but not enough to poison anyone," Gwen said, shuddering at the thought.

She had never tasted the adulterated milk. Her

uncle kept the farmhouse churn separate, and Gwen made sure she and her sister only ever drank from it, and not from any of the churns to be sent to the railway. But rumours abounded, and it was said there was not a farm in the valley where some unscrupulous practice did not take place.

"But they will poison someone – a delicate woman, a sickly child, and when they do…" Bryn said, shaking his head.

Gwen knew it was only a matter of time before Bryn was proved right and the thought made her shudder. Lamps were burning in the windows of the chapel, and the low playing of the organ could be heard coming from inside. They were practicing for Christmas, and as they entered the chapel, Reverend Llewelyn greeted them with a smile.

"Ah, my two youngest members. Have you been practicing your carols?" he asked, and Gwen and Bryn nodded.

"We have, yes, but it's different when we practice together," Bryn said.

"That's very true, indeed. Come now, take your places," he said.

Gwen smiled, glad to think she could forget her troubles for a few hours, caught up in the joys and pleasures of singing. Aled, along with several other labourers from the farm, was there, and they greeted Gwen and Bryn cheerily.

"We could have our own choir at the farm. We're all here, apart from the master and the two boys," Aled said, grinning at Gwen.

"And good riddance to them," another of the labourers said.

Gwen smiled. Her uncle was not popular amongst those who worked on the farm, and Cadell and Owain even less so. As they had grown older, both boys had become crueller, angrier, and more convinced of their own authority over others.

They lauded it over the labourers, ordering them about, and treating them with disdain, despite being half their age. In turn, the labourers mocked the pair incessantly, behind their backs, of course, and their impressions of Cadell and Owain always made Gwen laugh.

"Yes, good riddance to them. We don't want them here," Aled said as Reverend Llewelyn called for order.

"Good evening, everyone. We've got a lot to get through tonight, so let's not delay. We'll begin by practicing the carols for Christmas Day. We want a rousing rendition," he said, nodding to the organist, who now began to play.

"O come every Christian
to Bethlehem town now

To see how full of grace our God is;
O depth of such wonder,
the Godhead has prepared
An eternal promise of life:

Comes the King of creation
to deal with our weakness
Removing our suffering and load;
With no place to lodge in,
no dwelling, no bedroom,
A Christmas like that he was given."

It was a traditional Welsh carol, sung with gusto in the language of the valleys. Like so many other songs, Gwen knew the words by heart, as did the rest of the choir, and after two verses, Reverend Llewelyn called a halt, telling them to sing with a more pronounced tone.

"I want to hear the words, crisp like a mountain stream," he said.

Several of the labourers sniggered. The minister had a way of using metaphors without their meaning being fully communicated, and this was one.

"Are we to jump into the stream, too?" Aled whispered, and Gwen smiled.

But the choir had great respect for its choir master. Reverend Llewelyn was a kind and generous man, as dedicated to his flock as he was to God. He had ministered diligently in the valley for many years, his father having been a minister before him. He was a godly man, but not overly pious, and was as comfortable with the labourers and shepherds as he was with the landowners and farmers.

"Now, let's try the next two verses," Reverend Llewelyn said, raising his arms as though in the pose of a conductor.

"Give praise to the little Son,
on the knees of fair Mary,
The Godhead came a babe to our world:
His grace may we receive,
his merit to proclaim
And may we for ever serve Him."

The great Prince of peace,
at last he renews earth,
for us makes a place to live;
So don't stir up envy

*nor turmoil nor strife,
Our God plans to wear a crown."*

WHETHER NEXT VERSES of the carol had been sung in such a way as to appear "crisp, like a mountain stream" Gwen was uncertain, but Reverend Llewelyn appeared pleased, beaming at them, as he drew his fingers through the air in an elaborated movement of cessation.

"It's a beautiful carol," Bryn whispered, and Gwen nodded.

O Dued pob Cristion was one of her favourites, and she had fond memories of hearing her aunt sing it at Christmas in years gone past. Those days seemed distant, another world, and with another Christmas approaching, Gwen knew her life was not getting any easier.

She still saw to all the domestic chores at the farm, cooking, cleaning, keeping the fires going. She had her jobs on the farm too; milking the cows, feeding the herd, taking care of the chickens, and helping with the calving and lambing.

Her life was the same, day by day, the dull monotony of farm life broken only by the Friday night rehearsals, and the time she spent with Bryn.

"I'll see you on Sunday," she said as they filed out of the chapel after the rehearsal.

"Come up to the cottage for a bit. You don't have to go home just yet. Come and see my grandmother. She'd like to see you, she always does," Bryn said.

Gwen was grateful for the invitation. She liked Bryn's grandmother, the woman, "as old as the hills" as Bryn described her. She was over eighty years old and could remember back to before the turn of the century.

She had lived her whole life in the valley, never leaving its confines, and she knew everything about its myths and legends, its history, its past, and its present. Her cottage lay at the top of a winding track, high up in the woods. It was a steep climb, even for the agile valley dwellers. It had been her childhood home, and Bryn's own father had been raised there as a boy.

"Is there any bread and dripping? I'm ever so hungry," Gwen said as they made their way up to the cottage through the trees.

It was dark, but the moon was full, and the stars twinkled in the sky above, the moonlight casting long shadows from the trees. A lamp was burning in the window of the cottage, and as they approached, the door opened, and a voice called out into the darkness.

"Bryn? Is that you?" his grandmother called.

"It's me, Grandmother, and I've brought Gwen with me, too," Bryn called out.

They hurried up the last part of the slope, reaching the cottage as Bryn's grandmother came to the gate holding a lamp. Her name was Rhian, and Gwen looked up at her and smiled, marvelling at the strength in her ancient body. Her face was wrinkled, yet her eyes were bright and keen.

"It's nice to see you, Gwen. You're always welcome here. Come in and warm yourselves by the fire. I've the kettle boiling, and there's plenty of bread and dripping," she said.

Bryn led Gwen up the path to the cottage door, and they stepped into the parlour, where a bright fire was burning in the hearth. The cottage was small, but comfortable, with two beds built into alcoves in the wall.

A table and chairs stood in one corner, and a rocking chair stood by the hearth. The walls were lined with all manner of crafts–weavings, carvings, crude paintings–and a large rug covered the floor. Gwen liked to come to the cottage. She felt safe there, and now she sat down on the rug by the hearth to warm herself.

"Can I cut some bread, Grandmother?" Bryn asked, as his grandmother closed the door behind them.

"Cut it nice and thick, Bryn," she said, throwing another log onto the fire.

Bryn cut two large slices from a loaf on the table. The dripping dish was perched on a shelf next to the fire, and Gwen and Bryn spread their slices of bread liberally, smiling at one another as they began to eat. Bryn's grandmother made the tea, stewing it in the pot to be extra strong–just how Gwen liked it.

"We sang *O Dued pob Cristion* this evening, Grandmother," Bryn said, through a mouthful of bread and dripping.

"That's one of my favourites. A beautiful carol," she said, smiling at Gwen, who nodded.

"My aunt used to sing it to us when we were children," she said.

Although Gwen and Bryn had not known one another as small children, Bryn's grandmother and Gwen's aunt had been on friendly terms, and over the years, Bryn's grandmother had told her many stories about her aunt, and the kindnesses she had shown to so many in the valley.

"Your aunt had a beautiful voice, Gwen. It used to come over so strongly in the chapel on a Sunday morning. I could always tell when Cerian was there," Bryn's grandmother said.

She poured the tea, and Bryn cut two more thick slices of bread, spreading them liberally with dripping and handing Gwen the bigger piece. It had been snowing that day, and the wind was picking up, whistling through the trees, and rattling at the window frames. But the cottage was cosy, and the fire was bright. Bryn's grandmother had lit candles around the room, and together they talked long into the evening.

"I should be getting back to the farm. They'll be wondering where I am," Gwen said, for she had lost track of time, her eyes growing heavy in the comforting warmth of the fire.

"Bryn can walk with you," his grandmother said, and Bryn nodded.

He put on a scarf, and Gwen wrapped herself tightly in her shawl, for the night was cold.

"Thank you," Gwen said, saying goodbye to Bryn's grandmother.

"I think of you often, Gwen – and not just because you and Bryn are so close. You're so very much like your aunt. She died too young, and I've lived too long. Thank goodness we don't know God's reasons," she said, shaking her head.

But as she got to her feet, she was seized by a sudden fit of coughing, and she sat down heavily in the rocking chair with a sigh. Bryn hurried over to her with a look of concern on his face.

"Are you alright, Grandmother?" he asked, and she nodded.

"I'll be alright, Bryn. Just a little weakness, that's

all. Take Gwen home, then hurry back. I'll be in bed before long," she replied.

Gwen and Bryn made their way outside. Gwen held a lamp in her hand, and Bryn closed the door behind them, glancing at Gwen with a worried expression on his face.

His grandmother was usually a model of health. She still walked on the hills above the valley and carried buckets of water up the steep path from the spring below. Gwen had never seen any sign of weakness in her, even as she feared something was now wrong.

"I… let's get to the farm. I should come back quickly," Bryn said, and he hurried off down the path, with Gwen following behind.

"I'm sure she'll be alright, Bryn. It's just a cough," Gwen said.

Bryn nodded, turning to Gwen, and forcing a smile to his face.

"Yes… I'm sure she will be. She's as strong as an ox," he said, and Gwen nodded.

"Absolutely. You don't need to worry," she said, even as she herself *was* worried.

A fever, an illness, a sickness–it could seize a person without warning. The same had happened to Gwen's aunt. She had been a model of health, rosy-cheeked and robust, but a sudden chill had afflicted her, and a day later she had been confined to her bed.

The fever had risen, gradually overtaking her, and within three weeks, she was dead. Gwen knew the same thought would be on Bryn's mind, even as she did not dare to voice it herself.

"Gwen… will you come tomorrow, to see my grandmother, I mean?" Bryn asked and Gwen nodded.

"I'd be glad to. I can make some broth for her or bring a loaf of bread from the baker. Or I can sit with her whilst you run whatever errands you need to run," Gwen said.

She wanted to help. She wanted to repay the kindness of Bryn and his grandmother–the closest thing to family, apart from Madlen, she had. They walked in silence up to Talfryn Farm, but at the gate leading into the farmyard, they paused, and Bryn set down the lamp, the two of them leaning on the bars.

"I'm worried about her, Gwen," Bryn said, and Gwen nodded.

"I know you are. But she'll be alright. She's got you to look after her," Gwen said, slipping her hand into Bryn's and squeezing it reassuringly.

He nodded, and for a moment, they stood in silence by the gate. Gwen leaned forward and kissed him on the cheek, wanting to reassure him. He smiled at her and put his arms around her.

"I'll try my best," he said.

They parted ways, and Gwen watched as Bryn hurried down the lane, the lamp bobbing in his hand. She sighed, knowing there was a very real danger of tragedy, and fearing what would happen to Bryn if the unthinkable should occur.

"Gwen? Is that you? Get inside," a shout came across the farmyard, and Gwen looked up to see the outline of her uncle standing in the doorway to the farmhouse.

Reluctantly, she climbed over the gate, glancing again down the lane to where the bobbing lamp was disappearing into the trees. Her uncle shouted to her again, and sighing, she made her way inside, finding Madlen sitting on her own in a corner, whilst Cadell and Owain sat in front of the fire.

"Where have you been?" Cadell snarled.

"I was at the choir practice," Gwen replied.

"Until nine O'clock?" her uncle said, glaring at her as he closed the door and pulled across the bolt.

"I went to the cottage to see Bryn and his grandmother. She's not very well," Gwen replied.

Her uncle made no comment, sitting down in front of the fire and placing a slice of bread on the end of a toasting fork. Gwen went over to where Madlen was sitting in the shadows, and she put her arms around her sister and held her close.

"Come with me tomorrow to see Bryn and his grandmother," she whispered, and her sister nodded.

"I will do," she said, even as their uncle called out for more logs to be put on the fire, and a fresh pot of tea to be brewed.

* * *

THE NEXT DAY, having finished milking the cows and seeing to her chores around the house, Gwen set out for the cottage. She had made a simple broth of winter vegetables and barley. She and Madlen carried it between them, trying not to spill it as they made their way down the track from the farm to the cottage Bryn shared with his grandmother.

Smoke was rising from the chimney, and Bryn was outside chopping wood. As they approached, he looked up, and Gwen could tell immediately something was wrong.

"Bryn?" she called out, and he shook his head, setting down the axe and coming towards them.

"She's not well, Gwen. It's kind of you both to come, but she's not well. She took to her bed last night, but she didn't get up this morning. She keeps coughing–it's horrible to hear. I'm trying to keep her warm, but she's shivering, too," he said.

Gwen nodded, a sudden fear overtaking her. It was just as it had been for her aunt.

"We've brought you some broth, and Madlen can run down to the baker and bring some loaves," Gwen said.

"It's kind of you both. But I don't know if she can even eat. It's all happened so fast. You saw it for yourself," he said.

He led them to the door of the cottage, opening it tentatively. The fire was burning brightly, and Gwen could see the outline of Bryn's grandmother, covered with blankets, lying in the alcove where her bed was.

At the sound of the door opening, she raised her head, and Gwen and Madlen set the pan of broth down on the table before approaching the alcove as Bryn put fresh logs on the fire.

"Ah, Gwen... is that you? And Madlen, too?" Bryn's grandmother said.

Gwen took the old woman's hand in hers. It was cold to the touch, but her forehead was burning up. It was just as it had been for Gwen's aunt, and she was seized by a sudden fear, a premonition of what was to come.

"Yes, it's us. We've brought you some broth. And I'm going to send Madlen down to the bakery for some loaves of bread. We'll keep you warm. Bryn's chopping wood for the fire," Gwen said.

Bryn's grandmother nodded. She was struggling to sit up, even as Gwen tried to keep her lying down.

THE MILK MAID ORPHAN

"I want to get up, Gwen," she said.

"You need to rest. We're worried about you, Rhian," Gwen said, and the old woman gave a weak smile.

"You're a kind child, Gwen… your poor aunt," she said, and Gwen nodded.

"I'll stay with you. We both will," she said, glancing over her shoulder to where Bryn was standing in the doorway with an armful of logs for the fire.

He looked sad, as though he realised the inevitability of what was to come. Death came to everyone, and it seemed this was to be his grandmother's time. Gwen stayed at the cottage for the rest of the day, trying to keep Rhian comfortable as best she could. She sent Madlen to the bakery for the loaves of bread, and back to the farm to bring a small churn of milk.

"Uncle says you're to come back at once," Madlen said, setting the churn down on the table in the cottage.

Gwen was sitting at Bryn's grandmother's bedside, and Bryn was stoking up the fire.

"Can't he manage without me for half a day?" Gwen replied, for she had no intention of returning to the farm at her uncle's bidding.

Madlen shook her head.

"He was angry, Gwen, he and Cadell," Madlen

replied.

"Then let them be angry," Gwen said, glancing back at Bryn's grandmother, who was now half asleep, her breathing heavy and laboured.

Gwen had done all she could to make Rhian comfortable, but there was nothing more she could do. Bryn's grandmother had eaten a few spoonfuls of broth, but had refused any more, and had managed only to sip a little tea from a saucer Gwen had held for her.

Bryn had looked on sadly, and it seemed he did not know what to do. He was caught up in the grief of knowing the inevitable was not far off. His grandmother had raised him. She was his mother, and his grandmother–she was everything he had, apart from Gwen.

"Don't stay if you'll get into trouble," Bryn said, but Gwen shook her head.

"I want to stay, Bryn. You and your grandmother… you're like family to me," she said, and Bryn now came to sit next to her by the bedside.

They kept vigil for the rest of the evening, but the fever had taken hold, and Bryn's grandmother did not open her eyes again.

She died during the night, and Gwen sent Madlen to fetch Reverend Llewelyn at first light. Bryn was sitting quietly at his grandmother's side, his hand clasped in hers, and Gwen put her arm

THE MILK MAID ORPHAN

around him, knowing how he must feel, even as he remained silent.

"Shall we pray?" she said, and Bryn nodded.

Together, their eyes closed, and their hands together, they kneeled at the bedside in silent prayer, and it was in this posture they remained until Reverend Llewelyn arrived. He, too, said some prayers before telling them he had already taken the liberty of sending one of his servants to fetch the undertakers.

"Your grandmother was a good and godly woman, Bryn. Her loss will be felt by all of us in the valley," he said.

Bryn had not yet shed a tear, but now, his shoulders heaving, he wept. Gwen put her arms around him, the two of them clinging to one another at the bedside. Reverend Llewelyn expressed further sorrowful sentiments and assured Bryn he would do everything he could to help him in the coming days and weeks.

"But what am I to do?" Bryn asked, looking up through his tears.

His grandmother's cottage was a tied dwelling. It belonged to one of the farms, and Bryn would not be able to live there by himself. He was only a little older than Gwen herself, and now a look of despair came over his face. Reverend Llewelyn looked at him sympathetically.

"I'll do what I can to help you, Bryn. I promise. I'll speak to Mr. Thomas today. But for now, allow yourself time to mourn. I'll make sure the undertakers have all the arrangements in hand," he said, glancing again at the lifeless body of Bryn's grandmother on the bed.

Gwen stayed with Bryn for the rest of the day, sending Madlen back to Talfryn Farm to tell their uncle what had happened. Bryn was in shock, and Gwen promised she would do all she could to help him, just as others did, too, as news of Rhian's death spread through the valley.

Mourners came to pay their respects, and the undertakers arrived to carry the coffin down to the chapel of rest.

"She's at peace, Bryn," Gwen said, as they watched the coffin being taken away.

"She was so… strong," he said, and Gwen squeezed his hand in hers.

"I know she was, and we'll both miss her terribly," Gwen replied.

"I just… I don't know what I'll do," he said, turning to Gwen and shaking his head.

"It'll be alright, I promise," Gwen replied, and the two of them stood in silence, watching the slow progress of the coffin down the hill, the death of Bryn's grandmother marking the end of a chapter for them both.

THE SONG SCHOOL

Bryn's grandmother's funeral took place a few days later. It was a sombre affair, on a day when the valley was shrouded in low cloud, with snow lying thick on the ground. It was presided over by Reverend Llewelyn, who preached a long sermon on fidelity to Christian morals, using Bryn's grandmother as his example.

"She was as old as the hills, some might have said, and so, too, is our faith – an ancient and steady guide on the path of life," he had said.

Gwen had stood at Bryn's side, the two of them holding hands, watching as the coffin of Bryn's grandmother was lowered into the ground. They had thrown in handfuls of dirt, as was tradition, and listened to the prayers exhorting God to receive the soul of Bryn's grandmother into the peace of Heaven.

Afterwards, Gwen had accompanied Bryn home, but the cottage had felt cold and empty, devoid of the life Bryn's grandmother had given it.

"I don't know if I can stay here. It's up to Mr. Thomas, I suppose. I don't think he's going to let me. He only allowed my grandmother to stay here because of my grandfather," Bryn said, shaking his head sadly.

Bryn's grandfather had been a labourer on Mr. Thomas's farm down in the valley, but the cottage would be needed for other workers, and Bryn was still too young to take on such a job.

"I'm sure he won't force you to leave," Gwen said, but Bryn shook his head.

"Why wouldn't he? I don't have anywhere else to go," he said, sitting down at the table with a sigh.

Gwen was not used to seeing Bryn so despondent. He was usually so cheerful, and always with a song in his heart. She wanted to help him, even as she was uncertain how to do so.

"Perhaps… you could live on the farm with us. I could ask my uncle. He always needs labourers," Gwen said.

Bryn sighed.

"Yes… and adulterate the milk, I suppose," he replied.

Gwen sighed. Bryn was right, of course. But she could see no other way to help him, even as longed to do so.

"I'll speak to my uncle," she said.

She was loath to leave him, but he assured he would be alright, telling her he wanted some time to himself. Gwen made her way back to the farm, determined to do something to help Bryn, and summoning her courage, she approached her uncle, who was working in one of the barns. He looked up at her, narrowing his eyes as she cleared her throat.

"You're back from the funeral, then?" he said, for neither he nor Cadell had attended.

"A lot of people came. It was so sad," Gwen said, and her uncle waved his hand dismissively.

"She was ancient. It was her time. Unlike your aunt..." he said.

If there was any decency left in Gwen's uncle, it emerged whenever he spoke of her aunt. He had loved her–he still loved her–and her loss had caused him to turn into the bitter, angry man he now was.

"But she left Bryn behind, Uncle. He's devastated," Gwen replied.

"And why didn't she make provision for him? Didn't she realise she wouldn't last forever?" he said.

Gwen's uncle could be callous. He was a cruel man, devoid of pity for anyone but himself and his own loss. He had not once given comfort to Gwen after her aunt's death, treating her as a burden rather than a fellow mourner.

"Well… but… can't we do something to help him?" Gwen asked.

"And what do you think I can do for him?" her uncle snarled.

"Well… couldn't… perhaps he could live here with us. You said yourself the other day we need another labourer," Gwen replied, but her uncle only laughed.

"I meant a man, Gwen, not a boy. No, it's out of the question. I won't have another mouth to feed. Not when… no… I won't have it. If Rhian didn't make provision for her grandson, so be it. I won't be the one to take care of him. Aren't there any poorhouses? Any orphanages? I'm sure Reverend Llewelyn can make arrangements. I already have three cases of charity to see to," he replied.

He was referring to Gwen and her sister and brother, even as their uncle treated Owain as his own. It was a reminder of how fragile their existence at the farm truly was. They were there on their uncle's charity, and if he chose to send them away, he could…

"But…" she began, and her uncle raised his hand to her.

"Enough, Gwen. I won't hear any more. Let him

fend for himself. Better he learns to do so now, rather than later," he said, and Gwen sighed.

"Very well, Uncle," she said, shaking her head sadly.

But the matter of what was to become of Bryn remained, and in the coming days, his future became clearer, and bleaker.

"Mr. Thomas won't allow me to stay. He's given notice of a month on the cottage," Bryn said, as the two of them walked to the rehearsal at the chapel that Friday afternoon.

It was already getting dark, though the day had been clear, promising a cold and starlit night. Gwen had brought Bryn some bread and cheese from the farm, taking it from the table when her uncle was not looking, and now she sighed, feeling helpless as to what she could do to help him further.

"But… where does he expect you to go?" she said, and Bryn shook his head.

"I don't know–I don't know where I can go. There's nothing for me here," Bryn replied.

They had reached the gate to the graveyard, and the mound of earth marking the freshly filled in grave of Bryn's grandmother was clear to see on the far side–a stark reminder of how quickly circumstances could change.

"But… I don't want you to go," Gwen replied, and Bryn shook his head.

"But what can I do, Gwen?" he replied.

Lamps burned in the windows of the chapel, but only a small number had gathered for the rehearsal that night, the cold having kept many away.

"But we'll warm ourselves with the song of the Lord," Reverend Llewelyn was saying as Gwen and Bryn entered the chapel.

The organist was sitting waiting to play, and the other members of the choir, the few present, had taken their places at the front of the chapel. But when Reverend Llewlyn saw Gwen and Bryn, he beckoned them to one side.

"Shouldn't we get started, Reverend Llewelyn," Bryn said, but the minister shook his head.

"They can wait for a moment, Bryn. I've got some good news for you. I think I've found a solution to your problem, and to Mr. Thomas' lack of Christian charity. I've tried to impress the seriousness of the matter on him, but given your grandmother lived by grace and favour, perhaps it's inevitable he now wants to make a profit. At any rate, he'd made his decision," Reverend Llewelyn said.

"And what about the solution?" Bryn asked, for the minster had a habit of going off at tangents, rather than saying what he meant to say when he meant to say it.

"Ah… yes, forgive me. The matter in hand, yes, well… I discovered quite by chance, whilst perusing a church periodical, of the existence of a song school for talented singers in our tradition. The boys are housed and educated in return for singing chapel services in a local congregation. It's open to auditions and recommendations. You're a fine singer, Bryn. You've got a voice far beyond the range of most boys your age. You're an ideal candidate for the song school," Reverend Llewelyn said, and Bryn's eyes grew wide with astonishment.

"But that's wonderful, Reverend Llewelyn… I don't know what to say. And the school–it's near here, I presume? I'd sing here on a Sunday, in the chapel," Bryn said, but Reverend Llewelyn laughed.

"Near here? No, not at all. It's in London, Bryn. You'd go to London. I'm sure the congregation here would cover the expense, given the circumstances. I've already taken the liberty of writing to the headmaster. As it happens, we're old acquaintances. You'd be singing at the Welsh chapel in London. It's a chapel much like our own, though its congregation is quite different. It's a marvellous opportunity and seems to resolve your difficulties admirably. I'm afraid the only alternative would be… well, the poorhouse or the orphanage. I know where I'd rather be," he said.

Bryn nodded, glancing at Gwen, who could hardly believe what she had heard. It seemed remarkable, even as its implications were clear.

"What do you think?" Bryn said as Reverend Llewelyn called for the rehearsal to begin.

"I... it's a wonderful opportunity," Gwen said, even as it broke her heart to say so.

They both knew what the implications would be. Bryn would leave the valley for London, and it was unlikely he would return, not for a long time, at least.

"I've got to take the chance. There's nothing for me here. Well... I mean... I don't want to leave, but... what choice do I have?" Bryn replied.

There was no time for further conversation now, and they joined the depleted ranks of the choir for the practice. There was no doubting what Reverend Llewelyn had said. Bryn had a beautiful voice, and it rose loud and clear above the others, filling the chapel with God's praises.

At the end of the rehearsal, Reverend Llewelyn again asked Bryn for a decision, telling him he would to the headmaster of the song school the very next day.

"You can be there next week. They take new pupils at any time of the year. It's your chance, Bryn. London, with all its grandiose opportunities, and an education you could never hope for here," he said.

It was an immense kindness, and Bryn agreed to Reverend Llewelyn making the recommendation. Gwen and Bryn walked home in a sombre mood.

They both knew the change that was about to happen, a change set to alter both their lives immeasurably. Gwen had imagined Bryn would always be there, the two of them growing up together, and perhaps even...

"I can write to you," Bryn said, as they walked up the track towards the farm.

"And I'll write to you, too," Gwen replied.

"And... well, it won't be forever, I suppose. I'll come back. I'm sure I'll come back," he said, as though recognising her fears.

"I'm sure you will," Gwen said.

She did not want him to feel guilty, nor did she want to dissuade him from going. Her uncle had forbidden any further talk of Bryn living at the farm, and with Mr. Thomas having given him just a few weeks to find another place to live, Bryn had no choice but to accept Reverend Llewelyn's generous offer.

Despite not wanting to hold him back, Gwen knew how much she would miss him, and now, as they came to the gate, she fought back the tears rising in her eyes.

"Gwen, I... I'll miss you terribly, and Madlen, too. I... it won't be forever. But I've got to go. There's nothing left for me here–no job, nowhere to live. Only you..." he said, and Gwen took his hand in hers.

"I don't want to hold you back. You've got to go. You can't stay here," she said, and he nodded.

"I'll come up tomorrow. We can talk more about it then," he said, and he put his arms around her, the two of them embracing in silence.

As he stepped back, Gwen brushed a tear from her eye and sniffed.

"Well… I'll have to improve my singing, too. Perhaps I can come to the song school," she said, forcing a smile to her face.

"I think it's only for boys," Bryn replied.

"I… you've got to go, but we'll always be friends, won't we?" Gwen said, and Bryn nodded.

"Always," he replied, and leaning forward, he kissed her on the cheek.

As Gwen watched him go, it felt as though another chapter in her life was closing. She had lost her aunt, and now she was about to lose her best friend, too. A tear ran down her cheek, and she sighed, knowing the coming months and years would only grow harder.

A TEARFUL FAREWELL

Bryn's departure for London happened within a week of Reverend Llewelyn making his suggestion of the song school. The minister had written to the headmaster, recommending Bryn for the school, and a reply had been hastily delivered, informing Reverend Llewelyn his letter had been an answer to prayer.

"Several of the children are struck down with illness, and without extra numbers, the future of the choir appears in jeopardy," Reverend Llewelyn had read, holding out the letter to Bryn, as he and Gwen stood in chapel a few days later.

"So, I'm to leave at once?" Bryn had said, and Reverend Llewelyn nodded.

"As soon as the arrangements can be made," the minster had replied.

A train ticket was purchased at the expense of the congregation, and Bryn packed up his meagre possessions, bringing them to the farm where Reverend Llewelyn was to collect him in his horse and cart for the journey to the station–the path to the cottage being too steep for horses.

"I've made you some sandwiches for the journey," Gwen said, handing over a brown paper packet neatly tied with string.

Bryn thanked her, putting the sandwiches in to his pocket, before glancing down the track for any sign of the minister.

"I think I've got everything. There wasn't much to pack. Mr. Thomas told me he'll clear the cottage of my grandmother's possessions, and I suppose… well, that's it, isn't it?" Bryn said, and Gwen nodded.

"I'll tend the grave when I go to visit my aunt's," she said, and Bryn sighed.

"It won't be forever, Gwen. I'll come back. And I'll write to you, I promise. And Reverend Llewelyn can help you with the reading and reply. He could teach you," Bryn said.

Gwen had been practising, but she still found reading and writing difficult. But she was determined to learn, just as she was determined the two of them would keep in touch.

"We won't lose touch, I promise. And perhaps… well, perhaps I could even come to London and see you," Gwen said, for she had always imagined what it would be like to ride the milk train through the valleys and across the country to the capital.

In her mind, London was an endless metropolis. A place to be feared, even as it fascinated her.

"I'll tell you everything. It's going to be exciting. But... I'll miss you, Gwen," Bryn said, reaching out his hand to take hers.

But at that moment, a sneering jeer came from across the farmyard, and Cadell appeared from one of the barns, accompanied by Owain.

"How touching," he said, as Gwen and Bryn turned to face him defiantly.

"Go away," Gwen said, as her cousin and brother advanced towards them.

"No, Gwen, I won't go away. It's my farm–you're the one who should leave. Why don't you go with him?" Cadell said, and Owain laughed.

"Yes, Gwen, you go with him," he said, mimicking their cousin's cruel tones.

Gwen shook her head. Her brother repulsed her. He had become just like her uncle and cousin, and if she could have gone with Bryn, she would gladly have done so.

"Leave us alone," she said, as Reverend Llewelyn's horse and cart appeared along the track.

"Yes... you won't escape so easily, will you,

Gwen? Come along, Owain, we've got the churns to prepare," Cadell said.

This was his way of saying they were going to adulterate the milk, and it made Gwen shudder to think of it. She was glad her uncle had not given Bryn a job at the farm. He would only have been forced to take part in the wicked practices going on in the diary, and for this, at least, she was thankful. Bryn shook his head.

"I'm sorry to be leaving you with such… wicked men," he said.

"Owain isn't a man, and nor is Cadell. They're pitiful excuses. But my cousin's right, I won't escape so easily. I've got Madlen to think about, and even if we could escape, where would we go?" Gwen said.

She had thought the matter over a great deal, even as she knew there was no choice but for them to remain at Talfryn Farm. Circumstances prevented anything else, and Gwen knew her uncle needed only a single excuse to send them to the poorhouse or the orphanage.

As Reverend Llewelyn drew up in the cart, Gwen knew she was about to be left alone, her dearest friend now leaving her. It was a bereavement and tears welled up in her eyes.

"Gwen… you'll be alright, I promise. Please… don't cry," Bryn said, as tears rolled down Gwen's cheeks.

"I'll miss you so much," she said, throwing her arms around him and embracing him.

"And I'll miss you, too. And whenever I go to sing, I'll think of you, I promise. I'll think of all the songs we've sung together. And if you do the same, we'll still be close to one another, won't we?" he said, and Gwen nodded.

"Yes… you're right. We will," she replied.

"Come along, Bryn. We don't want to miss the train," Reverend Llewelyn called out, and Bryn stepped back, his hand still clasped in Gwen's, tears rolling down his cheeks, too.

"You've got to go," she said, and Bryn nodded.

"I'll write to you as soon as I get there," he said, throwing his bag onto the back of the cart and climbing up next to the minister on the board.

Madlen emerged from the milking shed, and she and Gwen ran alongside the cart as it trundled back down the track. They followed it until it turned out onto the wider bridleway leading down the valley towards the station.

They could no longer keep up, breathless from their exertions, and Bryn now turned to them and waved.

"I won't forget you," he called out, as tears rolled down Gwen's cheeks.

"I won't forget you, either," she called out,

watching as the horse and cart disappeared into the distance.

Madlen slipped her hand into Gwen's.

"Will he come back?" she asked.

Gwen nodded. She wanted to believe he would–she felt certain he would–even as she knew those who left the valley rarely returned. Life was changing in the outside world, the revolution of industrialisation was taking place, and many of the labourers, including those on her uncle's farm, had left to pursue new opportunities in the factories and mills of the north and east.

"I'm sure he will. He's going away to school. It's like boarding, I suppose," Gwen said, shivering and pulling her shawl tightly around her shoulders.

It had been snowing again, and dark clouds were gathering on the horizon, threatening further falls. Gwen and Madlen made their way back to the farm, taking refuge in the milking shed in the hope of avoiding Cadell and Owain.

"What are we going to do, Gwen? Will we live here for the rest of our lives?" Madlen asked.

Gwen did not know what to say. She hoped they would not, even as the future stretched out bleakly before them. Her own hopes and dreams, if she had ever had any, were dashed.

She had put her store in Bryn, and now he was gone. The world was moving on, but Gwen felt left behind. Their uncle could send them away at any moment, and she felt certain his threats would be realised if she or her sister put a foot out of line.

The threat of exposure hung over her uncle, too, and it was surely only a matter of time before someone discovered the truth as to what was happening with the adulterated milk.

"I don't know, Madlen. Not forever, I hope. But what else do we know but this? We don't have anywhere else to go, do we?" Gwen said, and Madlen shook her head.

"I wish Bryn had stayed," she said, and Gwen sighed.

"I wish he'd stayed, too. But… well… he had to go. It was the only place for him," Gwen said, determined not to cry or feel sorry for herself.

Bryn had not left out of spite. He had had no choice, even as Gwen knew she would miss him terribly.

"Gwen… you won't… leave me, will you?" Madlen asked, and Gwen shook her head.

"No, Madlen, I won't leave you. I promise," Gwen said, putting her arms around her sister, who began to sob.

Madlen was all she had left, and Gwen could not imagine being without her sister. Madlen was her only true friend. They had endured so much together, and now they would endure this loss, too.

"What are you two doing hiding in here?" their uncle said, pulling open the door of the milking shed to find them embracing.

Gwen turned to look at him, wiping the tears from her eyes.

"We... we were comforting one another," she said, and her uncle sneered.

"He's gone, Gwen. Reverend Llewelyn did what was best. If you don't like it, why don't you leave, too? You'd save me a mouth to feed, and you, too, Madlen," he snarled.

"Where would we go?" she asked, and her uncle shrugged.

"I don't care, Gwen, but as long as you're here, you work for your bed and board. Do you understand me? There's brass to polish inside, and the fire to lay. Madlen, bring in some logs for the store, then check on the hens. I won't have the two of you idling in here any longer," he said, pointing out of the milking shed with a threatening look on his face.

Gwen and Madlen did as they were told, following him out of the milking shed just as Cadell and Owain emerged from the dairy. They were always together. Owain was Cadell's shadow — an obedient puppy, kicked too many times. Her cousin sneered at Gwen, dusting the chalk off his hands as he did so.

"Has he gone?" he asked, and Gwen nodded.

"He's gone, yes," she replied, and Cadell laughed.

"I'm surprised you didn't go with him. Reverend Llewelyn could've married the two of you at the chapel on the way," he said, and Owain, too, began to laugh.

"Yes, Gwen, you're in love with him," he said, sneering at her in imitation of his cousin.

Tears welled up in Gwen's eyes, but she refused to give them the satisfaction of seeing her cry.

"Go away," she said, and the two of them laughed.

"You've got nowhere to go, Gwen. You and Madlen must stay here. Why don't you come and help us with the milk? There's still plenty of churns to fill," Cadell said, beckoning to Gwen, who shook her head.

"I won't… I won't be part of it," she said.

"You think yourself so high and mighty, don't you, Gwen? But you're no different from us. If it wasn't for the milk, there'd be no farm. The food you eat, the fire you sit in front of—it's all paid for with the chalk," Cadell said.

He was taunting her now, and Gwen turned away, refusing to listen to his wicked words, even as she knew they were true.

"I don't… I don't want to hear it," she said, even as her cousin advanced towards her, followed by Owain, who was laughing.

"You're as much a part of it as we are, Gwen.

There's no escaping it. Don't you see?" Cadell said, and he grabbed by the shoulder, forcing her to look at him.

"Let me go," she cried, pushing him away.

"Admit it, Gwen–you bear the same responsibility. If they come for us, they'll take you, too," he snarled.

"That's enough, Cadell. I don't want to hear anymore," Gwen's uncle said, but Gwen's anger was kindled, and now she lashed out, striking her cousin across the face, and causing him to fall back.

Owain gave a cry, charging forward, as though to attack Gwen. But Madlen seized hold of him, knocking him backwards to the ground, where he rolled in the snow and began to cry. Cadell was clutching at his cheek, and he glared at Gwen, who stood catching her breath, her face red with anger.

"I'm nothing like you," she cried, and seizing Madlen by the hand, she hurried her sister into the farmhouse, the two of them hiding upstairs for the rest of the evening.

With Bryn gone, and his grandmother dead, there was no longer any refuge for Gwen or her sister, and only the thought of singing in the chapel choir brought any sense of relief to the monotony of the coming days.

Gwen tried to keep herself busy, going about her jobs on the farm and avoiding her uncle, cousin, and

THE MILK MAID ORPHAN

brother as much as possible. She did not dare to enter the dairy, fearing what she knew to be there.

Her cousin was right. She was as much to blame in all of this as they were–complicit in her silence. It terrified her, and when next she entered the chapel for the rehearsal, a shudder ran through her at the thought of the day of judgement…

"Now… without Bryn here, we're facing some difficulties–we've got far too many tenors. I suppose that's the way of the valley choirs… Gwen, you come to this end of the row," Reverend Llewelyn said.

Gwen looked up in surprise to hear her name. She had been looking up at the ten commandments, written on a board above the wood cross on the communion table at the front of the chapel. She had read the same words over and over again– *"thou shalt not kill."*

She knew the terrible risks of adulterating the milk, and that a person could easily die from drinking the contaminated liquid. It terrified her to think of an innocent person drinking the milk her cousin had adulterated, and after the rehearsal was finished, she lingered at the back of the chapel, waiting for the minister, who smiled at her as he approached.

"Bryn caught his train on time. He'll be well settled in by now. I'm sure he'll write to you. When he does, bring it to show me. I'll read it for you and help you compose a reply," he said.

"That's very kind of you, Reverend Llewelyn," Gwen said, and the minister smiled.

"I know you miss him, Gwen. But he'll come back. It'll do him good. These men who live their whole lives in the valley… it's not good for them," he said.

"Reverend Llewelyn, I… if a person knows someone's doing something wrong, and they don't say anything about it, are they doing just as much wrong?" Gwen asked.

The minister looked at her in surprise.

"Good heavens, Gwen. Whatever are you talking about?" he asked, raising his eyebrows.

Gwen sighed, knowing she was betraying her uncle and cousin, and her brother, too. But she could not keep the matter to herself any longer, and without Bryn to confide in, Gwen felt she had only on choice in whom to tell.

"I… it's the milk at the farm, Reverend Llewelyn. It's filled with chalk," she said, and the minister nodded gravely.

"I see. And are you telling me this abhorrent practice is being performed by your uncle and cousin?" he asked.

Gwen nodded.

"And I know about it, but there's nothing I can do

about it, either. The food I eat, the warmth from the fire, the clothes I wear. It's all paid for with adulterated milk," she said, and tears welled up in her eyes as she spoke.

Reverend Llewelyn placed his hand gently on her shoulder.

"You've done the right thing in telling me, Gwen–though it's hardly a revelation. I doubt there's a farm in the valley that hasn't done something to make its milk go further. Often, they water it down, and that causes no harm to anyone, apart from the perpetrator's own conscience. But as for chalk... no, that's a different matter. Do you have reason to believe deaths have occurred because of milk from Talfryn Farm?" he asked, and Gwen shook her head.

She had no proof anyone had died because of the adulterated milk, but given it was sent to London, there was no telling either way.

"I don't know, but even the risk of it... it's too awful," she exclaimed, and Reverend Llewelyn nodded.

"You're still a child, Gwen. You're not responsible for your uncle's actions. You're not to blame for this, and as for being complicit... no, you're not to think of yourself in such a way, nor your sister, either. But what they're doing can't be allowed to continue," he said.

Gwen's eyes grew wide with horror, even as she knew Reverend Llewlyn was speaking the truth.

"Please, Reverend Llewelyn, if my uncle discovered I'd told you..." she stammered, knowing what her uncle would surely do to her if he knew she had even spoken of the matter.

"Don't worry, Gwen. I won't tell anyone. But I've got to do something about it. My own conscience won't allow me not to do so. It's a terrible situation, and if it was known for certain that someone had died. Well... your uncle and cousin would be responsible," he said.

Gwen glanced again at the ten commandments hanging on the wall at the far end of the chapel. There was no questioning what Reverend Llewelyn had told her. Her uncle was poisoning the milk, and if a person died because of him, the hangman's noose was what he deserved...

"I know... I just... what would happen to us? To Madlen and I?" Gwen asked, and Reverend Llewelyn sighed.

"Well... as I said, Gwen, you're not responsible for what they've done. You should go home now, though. And if anything else happens, come and tell me," he said.

Gwen walked home dejectedly. She did not know if she had done the right thing by telling Reverend Llewelyn the truth or not. She feared he might even confront her uncle, and even if he did not reveal the truth as to who had told him, the fact of it would be clear. As she stood at the farm gate, looking across the dark farmyard to the parlour window, where a solitary lamp was burning, she thought about running away–of never returning to the farm–even as she knew she could not do so.

"I'm not responsible for what they've done," she told herself, as she let herself into the farmhouse, but try as she might, Gwen could not rid herself of the fear she felt at the prospect of what was to come, knowing the discovery of the adulterated milk would bring consequences for them all.

THE MILK INSPECTORS

"And that's the last of them. That should see us through to March," Cadell said, heaving the last sack of chalk from the back of the farm cart.

The top opened as it landed on the ground, revealing the white powder inside, some of it spilling out onto the dirty snow covering the flagstones.

"Get those sacks into the dairy and don't let the chalk get damp. It'll turn the milk grey," Gwen's uncle shouted, and Cadell sneered.

"What does it matter? Grey or white, it's still the same, isn't it?" he said, shaking his head and laughing.

Gwen watched him take the first of the sacks, shouting at Owain to open the door to the dairy. It was the same every couple of months. Cadell would take the cart down the valley to one of the mines, purchasing the chalk from one of the workers who took a cut of the profits from the adulterated milk.

He did it brazenly, hardly bothering to disguise the fact of his errand, even as Gwen's uncle had warned him against becoming blasé.

"We can't afford to be discovered," he had warned him. Cadell was becoming complacent.

"You know what'll happen…" Gwen's uncle called out, but Cadell only laughed.

Gwen retreated to the milking shed, finding her sister tending to a sick cow lying in the straw.

"Is she still suffering?" Gwen asked, and Madlen looked up and nodded.

"I don't think there's anything more we can do for her. I think she likes the company, though. The poor thing, she reminds me of… well, when Bryn's grandmother died. She had the same look about her. It's like she's withdrawing from the world," Madlen said, and Gwen nodded, sitting down in the straw next to her sister and placing her hand gently on the creature's head.

The cow was warm to the touch, her eyes blinking rapidly, her mouth foaming.

"The poor thing," Gwen said.

They stayed with the animal for the rest of the afternoon, and as dusk was falling, Madlen went to fetch a lamp so they could keep vigil into the night.

"I won't leave her," she said.

Gwen stayed in the milking shed, stroking the cow's head, hoping the creature realised it was not alone. Her uncle would be angry to learn they had lost one of the herd, even as he did little to take care of them himself. She was about to go in search of Madlen, who had been gone for almost half an hour, when a commotion out in the farmyard caused her to prick up her ears.

"Cadell, get the cart ready... no, we'll go on foot. Bring Owain," her uncle shouted, and the sound of footsteps echoed on the still evening air.

Gwen went to the door, easing it open and peering out through the crack. To her astonishment, she saw Cadell and Owain hauling churns of milk out of the dairy. They were pouring it away, allowing it to spill out over the snow-covered ground. Madlen now came running from the farmhouse, the lamp she was carrying bobbing in the gathering gloom.

"Gwen!" she cried out, and Gwen pulled open the milking shed door, staring at her sister in astonishment.

"What's happened? Cadell and Owain are pouring away the milk," Gwen said, and her sister nodded.

"It's the milk board. They've made a raid on one of the farms at the far end of the valley. They're coming here next. One of their labourers just came to warn Uncle Dawid and Cadell. They're about to leave. They're certain they know the truth about the milk," Madlen exclaimed.

Gwen's eyes grew wide with fear. Reverend Llewelyn must have told the milk board what was happening in the valley. There had been rumours of inspections, but Talfryn Farm had so far avoided them, until now, that is.

"To leave? But where are they going?" Gwen replied.

"I don't know, but they're taking Owain, too," Madlen replied.

Gwen glanced back at the cow lying in the straw. There was nothing else they could do for the poor creature, even as it seemed the rest of the herd, too, was to be left to its fate. Gwen seized Madlen by the hand, and the two of them ran across the farmyard to the dairy, finding Cadell and Owain pouring away the last of the adulterated milk.

"And now the chalk. We'll spread it out across the snow. They'll walk across it, but they won't find it," Cadell said as he hauled one of the sacks he had brought up from the mine.

Owain ripped open the top, a cloud of white dust rising into the still evening air. He grabbed a handful of it, casting it out across the snow, where it fell like a fresh fall.

"What's happening?" Gwen said, but her cousin pushed her angrily away.

"You've got what you wanted, that's what's happening. Was it you? Did you tell the milk board what was happening? It wouldn't surprise me, you nasty little wench," he snarled.

Gwen stumbled back, and now her uncle came striding across the farmyard, dressed in his large overcoat, shouting for them to hurry up.

"Leave it. They already know. We need to leave. They'll be on the bridleway by now. We'll take the path through the woods across the top of the hill," he said.

Gwen had never seen her uncle look so terrified, his words frantic, his voice strained.

"What about the chalk?" Owain said.

"Leave it!" their uncle shouted, and he cuffed Owain hard across the back of the head.

Gwen and Madlen now watched as Cadell seized Owain's hand and dragged him across the farmyard towards the house.

"What are we going to do?" Madlen whispered.

Gwen did not know what they were going to do. Did her uncle expect them to come with him? Did he even want them to go with them? Gwen and Madlen did not have anywhere else to go, but nor did Gwen have any desire to go with her uncle, either.

She remembered Reverend Llewlyn's words,

knowing neither she nor her sister were responsible for what had been done to the milk, even as still feared they could be blamed.

"Hurry up. I think I can see lights on the bridleway. We need to leave now," Gwen's uncle called out, and Gwen and Madlen hurried over to the open door of the farmhouse.

"We're not coming," Gwen said, clutching Madlen's hand in hers. Her uncle looked at her with an angry expression on his face.

"You foolish child, you can't stay here," he exclaimed.

"Why not? We don't want to come," Gwen said, facing him defiantly.

"Leave them, Father. You said yourself we need to hurry," Cadell said, and Gwen nodded.

"Leave us. We'll fend for ourselves," she said. In truth she did not know what they would do, or how they would manage. All Gwen knew was she did not want to go with her uncle, wherever he, Cadell, and Owain were going.

"But… do as you please, we haven't got time for this," he said, seizing the last of the few possessions they had collected.

Gwen glanced at her brother. Now was the time for him to choose, even as she knew his choice was already made.

"Are you going, too, Owain?" Gwen asked, and hr brother nodded.

"Come along, there's no more time to waste," Cadell said, seizing Owain by the hand.

Now, Gwen and Madlen watched as their uncle, cousin, and brother hurried across the farmyard towards the path leading up into the woods beyond. The light of several lamps could now be seen clearly on the track leading up to the farm, and the sound of horse's hooves and men's voices echoed in the still night air.

"Gwen?" Madlen said, clinging tightly to Gwen's hand, the two of them watching as their uncle, cousin, and brother disappeared into the trees.

Gwen did not know what to do, even as they had made their choice. The others were gone, and they were the only ones left at the farm. The other labourers, too, had fled.

"Quickly… inside," Gwen said, for she did not know what would happen if they were discovered by the inspectors.

She had visions of the poorhouse, the orphanage, or worse. Despite Reverend Llewlyn's words, Gwen could not help but feel responsible for what had happened, and with her uncle gone, she feared she would be the one to take the blame.

They hurried into the farmhouse, finding the parlour in disarray. A solitary lamp stood on the table, next to the remnants of the evening meal, and the fire was burning low in the hearth. Gwen had always known where her aunt kept the housekeeping money, in a jar hidden in an alcove above the chimney recess.

She did not know if her uncle had known about it, though she after her aunt's death, Gwen had been too fearful of being caught to check…

"What are we going to do?" Madlen said, and Gwen hurried to the chimney, standing on one of the hearth stools and reaching up into the recess above.

A cloud of soot and dust showered down on her, but the jar was there, and reaching it down, she discovered it still contained the money her aunt had saved. She did not think it would be wrong to take it. Her aunt would have been horrified at the situation occurring around them, and Gwen slipped the money into her pocket, turning to find Madlen looking out the parlour window.

"What's happening?" Gwen asked, and Madlen pointed out into the darkness.

"They're here. Look," she said, and Gwen hurried over to the window, the two of them peering out fearfully into the farmyard.

Half a dozen men and two carts, pulled by large shire horses, had entered the farmyard. The gate wedged open with a discarded milk churn. They were calling out orders to one another, and three of them now entered the dairy, whilst the other three entered the milking shed.

Gwen put her arm around Madlen, her heart beating fast. She did not know whether to confront the men or for the two of them to hide. Either way, they would eventually be discovered. News of the raid would soon spread across the valley, and Gwen was convinced it was her words to Reverend Llewlyn that were responsible.

"They already know what's happened. They're just looking for proof," Gwen said.

"But how did they know? Someone must've told them," Madlen said.

"I did…" Gwen replied.

Her sister looked up at her in surprise.

"But Gwen…" she said, and Gwen sighed.

"Well… I told Reverend Llewelyn, and he must've told the milk board. After Bryn left, I didn't have anyone to confide in. I felt so guilty thinking about the milk. If someone dies… it doesn't bear thinking about," she said, shaking her head sadly.

But before Madlen could reply, a shout came from across the farmyard, and two of the men emerged from the dairy.

"There's chalk here, sacks full of it," one of them called out.

They had lamps with them, and two dogs, both of

whom were barking. Gwen and Madlen clung to one another fearfully, watching as the men approached the house.

"There's someone inside," another of them called out, and a moment later, there was a loud knocking at the door.

THE MILK TRAIN

Another knock, this time louder and more forceful, came at the door, and a voice called out from the step.

"Open up in there. It's the milk board. We're inspecting the farm. We know what you've been doing," a man called out.

Gwen went tentatively to the door, pulling back the bolt and opening it. There was no point in hiding, and she continued to remind herself she had done nothing wrong. The man was holding a lamp, its bright light shining in her eyes, and Gwen squinted, looking up as those gathered outside gave an exclamation of surprise, the dogs still barking loudly.

"It's just a child. Where's Dawid Parry? This is his farm, isn't it? If he's hiding, tell him to come out.

We're shutting this farm down," the man holding the lamp said.

"Please… he's gone… they've both gone, my uncle and cousin," Gwen stammered.

The man lowered the lamp. He was around the same age as her uncle, but with a beard and glasses, and now he squinted at her, surprised, it seemed, to discover her there.

"Gone? What do you mean? Did he know we were coming?" he said, and Gwen nodded.

"He knew, yes. They left in a hurry. They poured everything away. I'm here on my own with my sister," she said, and Madlen peered out nervously behind her.

"Terrible… leaving a child all alone… we'll have to tell Reverend Llewlyn they're here," the man said, but Gwen shook her head.

"No… please… we won't go. We don't want to go to the poorhouse or the orphanage. We want to stay here," she said, and the man laughed.

"Stay here? This farm doesn't belong to you, or your uncle. It belongs to the milk board. Do you know what your uncle's been doing?" he asked.

Gwen shook her head. She did not know the full extent of it, even as she had grasped the wickedness of it well enough. She had to keep reminding herself she was not to blame, even as she feared they would assume she was a part of her uncle's nefarious deeds.

"We don't know anything. They just left. He said the milk board knew, though," she said, and the man nodded.

"The milk board *does* know. We know just what your uncle's been doing. There have been some deaths linked to contaminated milk in London, adulterated with chalk. We've not been able to trace the farm specifically, but we know it's come from the valleys…" the man said, and now he barged into the parlour, followed by the other men who now began to conduct a search.

Gwen and Madlen stood watching, but Gwen knew they could not remain at the farm. She imagined what would happen when Reverend Llewelyn discovered they had been left alone. He would mean well, of course… telling them the poorhouse or the orphanage was the best place for them. Had Bryn not been possessed of a fine voice, he, too, might have ended up in just the same predicament.

"We have to get away," Gwen whispered, and Madlen looked up at her with a fearful expression.

"But where? We can't go through the woods like Uncle Dawid and the others," she said.

"Not through the woods, no—on the milk train," Gwen replied.

The thought had just occurred to her. There was nothing to keep them in the valley, and if they stayed, they would almost certainly be sent to the poorhouse or the orphanage.

The farm was now in the hands of the milk board, and Gwen feared the inspectors would seek to blame them–or at the least question them repeatedly–for their uncle's crimes.

"The milk train? But... where does it go?" Madlen replied.

"It goes to London, doesn't it? We'll go to London. We've got the money from Aunt Cerian's jar. We can use it to buy our tickets," Gwen replied.

She had not thought the matter through fully, and she knew it was madness to contemplate. But the alternative was far worse, and now Gwen's mind was made up.

"But when?" Madlen whispered.

"Now," Gwen replied, clearing her throat.

The inspector who had banged on the door looked up. The others were ransacking the parlour–opening draws, searching through papers, and turning the whole place upside down in search of further evidence against Gwen's uncle.

"What is it?" the man said.

"Please... there's a cow in the milking shed. It's very sick. We were sitting with it. It'll die, but it seems wrong to leave it alone," Gwen said.

The inspector nodded.

"Go and sit with it," he said, waving his hand dismissively.

"Let's go and get changed, Madlen," Gwen said, and they hurried upstairs, hastily changing into warmer clothes and wrapping themselves in several shawls.

"Are we going now?" Madlen asked, and Gwen nodded.

"Right now, yes. We don't have a moment to lose. We can catch the early train. It leaves long before sunrise," Gwen said.

The hoot of the train's horn was a familiar sound in the valley, and Gwen had often seen the puffs of smoke rising in the early morning during the summer when she was leading the herd in for milking.

The train took fresh milk to the capital, returning with empty churns to be filled again. It was the perfect means of escape if they could make it safely to the station.

"I'll get some apples from the store," Madlen whispered, and the two of them made their way back downstairs to the parlour.

The inspectors ignored them, and they hurried out into the farmyard, crossing to the milking shed under the cover of darkness. The cow was already dead and having stuffed their pockets with apples from the store, Gwen and Madlen hurried down the track towards the bridleway.

The night was cold, and they were glad of their shawls, clinging to one another's hands as they ran together as fast as they could.

"We need to get to the station quickly," Gwen said, even as she realised she did not know anything about catching a train, or what would happen when they reached the capital.

"Will we see Bryn?" Madlen asked, as they ran past the chapel, the graves in the graveyard silhouetted in the moonlight.

"I… I don't know… perhaps we will. I hope so," Gwen replied, even as she did not know where they would find him, or how they would contact him.

Everything lay open to questioning, but there was one certainty. They had to get away and do so as quickly as possible. As they came to the village, they paused to catch their breath. Talfryn was merely a hamlet – a small collection of houses built around the railway station.

Reverend Llewelyn lived there, and they crept past his house, keeping low below the hedge line lest they be seen. But it was still early, and on arriving at the station, they found only a couple of labourers loading milk churns onto one of the wagons.

The milk train took passengers in a single carriage

attached to the back of the engine, the wagons towed behind, and Gwen and Madlen went to the ticket office, peering over the counter in search of the stationmaster.

"Well now… this is a surprise," he said, appearing from a door behind them.

"Two tickets to London, Mr. Powell," Gwen said, for her aunt and the stationmaster had been friends, and Mr. Powell had often come to the farm for tea and griddle scones.

He looked at them curiously.

"To London? And why would the two of you be going to London? Does your uncle know about this?" he asked.

"Please, Mr. Powell," Gwen said, and now she explained their predicament, telling the stationmaster something of what had transpired over the previous hours.

He raised his eyebrows, his eyes growing wide as Gwen explained about the adulterated milk, tutting and shaking his head.

"Your uncle was never good to your aunt. She should've married me. I asked her… bless her, I asked her," he said, sighing.

"Please, Mr. Powell. Won't you sell us the tickets? If not for our sake, but hers," Gwen begged him.

"Yes, please, Mr. Powell. We don't want to go to the poorhouse or the orphanage," Madlen said, and the stationmaster shook his head.

"Alright. I don't want that. And I know your aunt wouldn't have wanted it, either. You can have the tickets, and if anyone asks, I'll tell them I haven't seen you," he said.

Gwen breathed a sigh of relief, handing over the money to Mr. Powell, but he refused to take it.

"We've got to give you something," she said, but the stationmaster would not hear of it.

"I don't need anything, Gwen. Your aunt was good to me when others weren't. I've never forgotten her. Keep the money. You'll need it when you get to London. And take care of yourselves. But hurry, now, they're stoking up the engine," he said, pointing out of the ticket office window onto the platform.

The engine was sending up plumes of steam, and the last of the milk churns had been loaded on. Gwen took Madlen's hand, the two of them waving to Mr. Powell as they boarded the train.

"Thank goodness, Madlen," Gwen said, as they sat down on the bare boards of the third-class compartment.

There was no one else on board, only the two of them, and now, with a blast of his whistle, the stationmaster waved his flag, and the milk train chugged out of the station, blasting its horn as a signal to the valley of its departure. Gwen could not help but marvel at the movement of the beast, its pistons turning, its wheels scraping against the rails, gathering momentum as it picked up speed along the track.

"How fast will it go?" Madlen asked.

"I don't know, faster than anything we can imagine," Gwen replied.

She pictured Bryn marvelling in the same way, and now she peered out of the window, watching the familiar landscape of the valley take on an entirely different look as they sped through it.

Dawn was breaking, and Gwen could see Talfryn Farm on the hill above, and Bryn's grandmother's cottage on the opposite side of the valley, and Mervgyn's Rock, and the chapel, and everything familiar to her now about to disappear.

"How will it stop?" Madlen asked, a note of panic now entering her voice as the train picked up speed.

"In the same way it began, I suppose," Gwen replied, though she did not know how the train could possibly stop, given how fast they were now travelling.

The track wound its way through the valley, emerging suddenly between the two hills at the far end. Such a journey would be a day's walk, at least, but it had been accomplished in just a few minutes, and Gwen continued to gaze out of the window, marvelling at the sight of the now unfamiliar landscape passing them by.

"I don't like it," Madlen said, and Gwen smiled.

"You'll get used to it," she replied, although even she herself was feeling somewhat queasy from the motion of the train.

Gwen sat down, putting her arm around Madlen, who rested her head on her shoulder.

"What will it be like? In London, I mean," Madlen said.

Gwen shook her head. She did not know what London would be like. She imagined a vast city, filled with the hustle and bustle of the metropolis. There would be tall buildings, gas lamps, men in top hats, hansom cabs, and fashionably dressed women. It would be like stepping into another world–a world far bigger than any they had known or been used to.

Already, their uncle's farm, the valley, their former life, seemed like a distant dream, even as the future remained uncertain.

"I don't know, but it'll certainly be very different from anything we've known before," Gwen replied.

"And where will we go once we get there?" Madlen asked.

Again, Gwen did not know the answer to her sister's question. She had no plan, and no idea of what would happen to them once they reached London. She had the vague idea of finding Bryn, but all she knew was he sang at a Welsh chapel and attended the song school. She did not have an address for him, for she had not yet received a letter from him, nor sent one to him.

"I... I don't know, Madlen. But we'll find our way. We've escaped–that's all that matters," Gwen said, telling herself everything would be alright, even as she could not be sure it would be.

"Will they look for us?" Madlen asked, but Gwen shook her head.

"I doubt they'll care much for where we are. It hardly matters, does it? We're not responsible for the adulterated milk. They were searching for evidence against Uncle Dawid. They said themselves–we're only children," she said, and Madlen nodded.

"And what about Uncle Dawid? Where's he gone?" Madlen asked.

Gwen had half expected to find her uncle on the train, but there had been no sign of him or the others at the station, and she felt certain Mr. Powell would have told her if he had been on the train.

She pictured the three of them hiding in the forest, lying low until they could make their escape. She shuddered to think what their fate would be if they were caught, and despite her feelings towards Owain, Gwen could not help but feel a certain sorrow at the thought of her brother being mixed up in such wickedness.

"They'll be hiding somewhere–the three of them.

They might take a train from the next valley or lie low for a while. Wherever they go, I just hope we don't meet them. I never want to see Uncle Dawid or Cadell again," Gwen replied.

"Or Owain," Madlen said.

Gwen sighed.

"Poor Owain–he made his bed, and now he's lying in it," she said.

The sun had now risen over the tops of the hills, and on either side of the train, a long, winding valley stretched out, its slopes wooded with bare-branched trees. A river, sparkling in the sunshine, wound its way on one side of the train, and Gwen leaned forward, resting her arms on the sill of the window, and gazing out at the passing landscape.

Madlen fell asleep at her side, and Gwen, too, grew tired, closing her eyes and allowing herself to drift into a dreamless sleep.

* * *

THE SHRILL BLAST of the train horn woke her, and she sat up, rubbing her eyes, the train having come to a halt.

"Where are we?" Madlen asked, for she, too, had been awoken by the sound of the train horn.

"I don't know," Gwen replied.

Gwen peered out of the window, uncertain as to

what was happening. She could see a red brick wall in front of them, towering to such heights she could not see above it. It was the same on the other side, as though the train was passing through a ravine.

Gwen did not know how long she had been asleep for, nor how far they had come in that time. The horn sounded again, and now the train pulled forward, chugging loudly, as darkness suddenly surrounded them.

"Gwen? What's happening?" Madlen exclaimed as the darkness engulfed them.

She put her arms around Gwen, the two of them clinging to one another in the pitch darkness. The horn sounded again, its shrill blast magnified in the confined space, and Madlen let out a cry.

In a sudden burst of light, the carriage was illuminated, and Gwen realised they had passed through a tunnel, emerging now onto an embankment with views out across…

"London!" Gwen cried out, and Madlen looked up, her eyes growing wide with astonishment.

From the top of the embankment, they could see the city stretching out before them, the roofs of the houses pitched in a jumble of slates and tiles, punctuated by the spires and steeples of the city's churches. Towering above it all was the dome of Saint Paul's cathedral–a sight Gwen had never imagined she would see, except in the pages of a picture book. The city seemed to stretch endlessly on a vast metropolis, just as she had imagined it to be.

"Is it really London?" Madlen asked, and Gwen laughed.

"Where else could it be, Madlen? Yes, this is London. We've made it. I can hardly believe it," she replied.

She imagined Bryn gazing out at the same view, marvelling at the same sights, and with the same anticipation in his heart. Bryn had known where he was going. There would have been someone to meet him, and a carriage or cab to take him to the school.

The train now slowed once again, and they pulled into a vast station, covered by an immense arched roof, like a cathedral, though built with iron and girders.

"It's astonishing," Gwen whispered, overawed by the sight, as now the train came to a halt on one of the platforms.

The station was crowded with people hurrying back and forth about their business, and shouts now came to unload the milk churns from the wagons.

"What do we do now?" Madlen asked.

Gwen did not know, but she knew they could not remain on the train, and pulling her shawls tightly around her shoulders, she took Madlen's hand and led her from the carriage.

As they stepped down from the train, they

narrowly avoided a man carrying a milk churn. He scolded them, and hurrying across the platform, they took shelter beneath a flight of steps, watching as the rest of the churns were unloaded.

"This one's for Claridge's," a man called out, pointing to a trolley of churns.

Gwen shuddered, wondering if milk from her uncle's farm was amongst those delivered that day. They had sent milk down to the station the previous morning, and some of it would not have been loaded until today.

"We can't stay here much longer. Someone's going to ask us what we're doing. We don't want to end up being taken away now we've escaped," Gwen said, and Madlen nodded.

"What about Bryn? Couldn't we ask someone if they know him?" she said, and Gwen smiled.

Her sister, it seemed, had not grasped the size and magnitude of the capital, and unlike the valley, no one knew anyone else.

"I don't think anyone will know him, Madlen. But we could try to find the song school, or the chapel where he sings. We've got Aunt Cerian's money. Let's get something to eat. We'll feel better then," she said, and taking Madlen's hand, she led her across the station concourse.

No one gave them a second glance, and they purchased two mutton pies from a stallholder by the entrance and sat on the steps to eat them. Around them, the hustle and bustle of the city was relentless.

Hansom cabs vied for space with carriages and horse and cart, whilst crows of people surged back and forth, jostling, and pushing one another along. Street sellers were plying their wares, calling out for those around them to buy everything from flowers, roasted chestnuts, the day's newspapers, and tots of gin and rum.

"I've never seen anything like it," Madlen said, and Gwen shook her head.

"Neither have I. It's quite something, isn't it?" she said, marvelling at the sights and sounds around them.

"What do you think Bryn's doing now?" Madlen asked, and Gwen shook her head.

She had lost track of the days, even as she realised it was now Sunday, for the bells of the surrounding churches were ringing out a merry peel.

"Oh… it's Sunday, isn't it? He'll be singing in the Welsh chapel. Perhaps we could find it," Gwen said, seized with a sudden hope and possibility.

If they could find Bryn, he might be able to help them, or know someone who could. Gwen's only plan had been to get away, and now they had done so, she was at something of a loss to know what to do next. Bryn was their only hope, and now they set about asking those around them for directions.

"Excuse me... excuse me... pardon me..." Madlen said, but everyone whose attention they tried to attract ignored me.

"We're looking for the Welsh chapel," Gwen said, but she was pushed aside by a man hurrying down the station steps, who glared at her as he passed.

"Out of my way, urchin," he exclaimed, before clambering into a waiting hansom cab.

Having been ignored by several others, the thought of their taking a hansom cab now occurred to Gwen. They had the jar of money belonging to their aunt, though Gwen did not know how much it equated to, or if there would be enough to get them to where they wanted to go.

"We could take a hansom cab, Madlen," she said, and her sister looked at her in surprise.

"Really?" she said, and Gwen nodded.

"Yes – we'll use the money in the jar. Come along. I don't think anyone's going to stop for us," she said, taking Madlen by the hand.

A line of hansom cabs stood at the bottom of the station steps, and well-dressed gentlemen were continually hurrying to claim them, calling out destinations across the capital to the drivers, who clicked their horses into motion and set off at speed.

Gwen and Madlen were pushed out of the way

several times, but an eventual lull in the process allowed them to catch the attention of one of the drivers, who looked at them suspiciously.

"What do you want?" he snarled.

"To go the Welsh chapel," Gwen said.

"And do you think I'll take you there on charity?" he replied.

Gwen shook her head, and reached into her pocket, pulling out the jar of money, and held it up to the driver, whose eyes grew wide with astonishment.

"Will that be enough?" she asked, and he nodded.

"That's enough," he said, a slight smile coming over his face as he spoke.

They climbed into the hansom cab, and the driver flicked the whip, clicking his tongue for the horse to move, and they set off with a jolt. Gwen slipped her hand into Madlen's, glancing at her sister and giving her what she hoped was a reassuring smile. She knew Madlen was scared, but they had one another, and that was all that mattered.

"We'll find Bryn, I promise," Gwen whispered, and Madlen nodded.

"And then what?" she asked, but Gwen did not know.

"One thing at a time, Madlen. One thing at a time," she replied.

THE WELSH CHAPEL

The hansom cab raced through the streets of London, passing along wide streets, flanked by grand buildings, some of them recognisable from pictures Gwen had seen of the capital, or stories she had heard others tell.

"I think we're in Trafalgar Square," Gwen said, as they passed the tall column on the top of which stood the proud figure of Admiral Nelson.

"Everything's so big, isn't it?" Madlen replied.

"Just think of the buildings as the hills, and the streets as the rivers," Gwen said, even as she, too, felt somewhat overwhelmed by the vastness of the capital.

It was a seemingly endless sprawl of streets and buildings and crowded beyond anything she had ever imagined. Back in Wales, only the odd farm cart, or labourer, passed along the track leading up to the farm, and days could go by without any visitors. Here, the crowds were relentless, and the traffic was like a fast-flowing river, carrying everything along in its wake.

"I hope we find Bryn," Madlen said, and Gwen nodded.

"I hope so, too," she replied, squeezing her sister's hand in hers.

The hansom cab now turned towards Buckingham Palace, the royal standard fluttering in the breeze above the vast edifice. Gwen gazed at it in amazement, imagining what it would be like to go inside.

"Is that where the Queen lives?" Madlen asked.

"That's right, and when the royal standard flies, it means she's at home," Gwen replied, remembering something Reverend Llewelyn had once told her.

Madlen's eyes grew wide with astonishment as the hansom cab raced past the iron railings, the guards at the gates resplendent in their red uniforms.

"Will we see her?" she asked, and Gwen smiled.

"I don't think we will, no," she replied.

Now they crossed a park, and Gwen was relieved to see some greenery, though the trees were bare.

"How much further is it?" she asked, calling out

to the cab driver, who turned and pointed his whip up ahead.

"Not much further. About a mile or so," he said, and Gwen nodded.

She did not know what to expect, only that the chapel would be a far cry from that where Reverend Llewelyn and the members of the choir would be gathering now for the Sunday service. She wondered how far the news of the milk board's raid had spread, and whether her uncle and the others had yet been apprehended.

"They'll have realised we're missing by now," Gwen said, and Madlen looked at her fearfully.

"Will they come looking for us, do you think?" she asked, and Gwen shook her head.

"How would they find us? It would be like looking for a needle in a haystack. They'll never find us here," she replied, squeezing Madlen's hand in hers.

Emerging from the park, the cab now turned down a side street, the crowds lessened, and the traffic calmer.

"Here it is, the Welsh chapel," the driver said, as they pulled up outside a plain red brick building with an arched window built high over the double doors.

"How much do we owe you?" Gwen said, opening the jar of money.

The cab driver reached over and took out one of the notes.

"That should do it," he said, grinning at Gwen, who was not entirely convinced she had not just been taken advantage of.

"Thank you," she said, helping Madlen down to the ground.

The hansom cab pulled away, leaving them at the bottom of the steps leading up to the door. The sound of music was coming from inside–singing– and a polished brass plaque next to the door indicated they had come to the right place.

"Welsh Chapel," Madlen read, and Gwen smiled.

She imagined Bryn inside–his voice part of the chorus they could hear echoing out onto the street. It was a rousing rendition of a hymn she knew well.

> *"Guide me, O thou great Redeemer,*
> *Pilgrim through this barren land;*
> *I am weak, but thou art mighty;*
> *Hold me with thy powerful hand:*
> *Bread of heaven, bread of heaven*
> *Feed me till I want no more.*
> *Feed me till I want no more."*

"Come on, let's go inside," Gwen said, taking Madlen's hand and leading her up the steps to the door. As she opened it, the sound of the music became louder. The hymn sung with such gusto as to transport Gwen back to the chapel in the valley, where she and Bryn had often sung together.

"Open thou the crystal fountain
Whence the healing stream shall flow;
Let the fiery, cloudy pillar
Lead me all my journey through:
Strong deliverer, strong deliverer
Be thou still my strength and shield.
Be thou still my strength and shield."

The chapel was vast, far larger than the exterior suggested, with a ceiling stretching high up above them, bordered by a gallery into which was packed several hundred people. The wooden pews below were similarly occupied, and at the front of the chapel stood the choir of men and boys.

A minister stood to one side in a preaching gown, and the choir was conducted by a tall man with a red face and large, handlebar moustache. It was not the chapel, nor the congregation, nor the minister that caught Gwen's eye, but the sight of someone she knew very well indeed.

"Look, Madlen, it's Bryn," Gwen whispered, pointing to where Bryn stood with the other boys in the centre of the choir.

It had only been a short while since she had last set eyes on him, but somehow, he appeared more grown up than before, dressed in a white robe with a collar, his hair combed back, and his eyes fixed on the conductor, who now guided the choir into the final verse.

"When I tread the verge of Jordan,
Bid my anxious fears subside;
Death of death, and hell's destruction,
Land me safe on Canaan's side:
Songs of praises, songs of praises
I will ever give to thee.
I will ever give to thee."

As the music came to an end, the minister stepped forward.

"Dearly beloved brethren, the scriptures moveth us to offer our praise and worship to God our heavenly father. As we have lifted our voices to heaven, so we lift our hearts in prayer, too," he said, joining his hands together.

The congregation did the same, their heads bowed, and Gwen and Madlen slipped into an empty pew at the back. Gwen looked up, trying to catch Bryn's eye. The rest of the choir had also sat down, and she could not now see him amongst the others.

The period of silent prayer now came to an end, and the minister rose to his feet, offering a final prayer, and giving notices for the coming week. He mentioned the song school, thanking the headmaster and choirmaster for their sterling efforts, despite the trouble of illness amongst some of the boys.

The final hymn was announced, but it was an unfamiliar one to Gwen, and she and Madlen stood silently at the back, watching as the choir gave voice to the tune.

"How will we speak to him?" Madlen asked, as the service came to an end.

"I'm not sure," Gwen said, but she was determined to do so – they had come too far to give up at the final moment.

As the sound of the organ died away, there was a general shuffling, and whispered voices rose all around them. The congregation filed out, and the minister left the chapel by a side door marked "vestry." The boys in the choir were called to order

THE MILK MAID ORPHAN

by the choirmaster, and Gwen could now see Bryn, albeit with his back to her.

"We'll return to school for luncheon, then back to rehearse here in the chapel later this afternoon. Some of you weren't paying attention to me this morning. A choir can only sing in harmony if its members behave as a harmony. That means always watching me as your conductor," the choirmaster said, looking pointedly at several of the boys, who hung their heads–whether out of shame or to disguise their obvious giggling.

"Let's wait for him by the main door," Gwen said as the choir now filed out along the main aisle of the chapel.

The two girls hurried out onto the steps, and Gwen watched anxiously as the first of the boys emerged. They were laughing and joking to one another, amused, it seemed, at their telling off by the choirmaster.

"Mr. Jones meant you, Myfanwy. You never look at him. Don't you like his moustache?" one of them said, and the others laughed.

"I do so look at him. I just look away when he's not looking at me," Myfanwy replied, and all of them roared with laughter.

Gwen and Madlen went unnoticed, and Gwen wondered where Bryn could be. But suddenly he emerged, talking earnestly to a tall, blonde-haired boy, the two of them leaning close to one another so Gwen could not hear what they were saying.

"Bryn?" she said, and Bryn looked up, startled, it seemed, to hear his name mentioned.

He stared at Gwen and Madlen in astonishment, pausing mid-sentence, as the blonde boy looked at him in surprise.

"Gwen? Madlen? What are you doing here?" he exclaimed, and Gwen blushed, fearing he would think her foolish for having done what she had done.

"I… it's a long story," Gwen said, even as a shout came from up ahead.

"Keep up at the back, there. Stop dawdling," the choirmaster called out.

"I don't have much time. Do you know where the song school is?" Bryn said, and Gwen shook her head.

"We don't know where anything is," she said, desperation now rising in her heart at the thought of their being separated again.

"It's about half a mile from here, on Saint James' Place. I'll meet you there tonight, at eight O'clock. Come to the door at the back. You'll find it easily enough," he said, and Gwen nodded.

The choirmaster called out again for the dawdlers to hurry up, and with a last look, Bryn hurried on, questioned immediately by his companion as Gwen and Madlen remained standing in the doorway of the chapel. Gwen watched as Bryn and the other boys disappeared. She did not know what she had expected, even as she feared losing him again.

"What do we do now?" Madlen asked, and Gwen sighed.

"I don't know. We'll have to wait until tonight, won't we?" she said, for it seemed there was nothing else they *could* do.

The day was cold, and a dusting of snow lay over the roofs and pavements. Gwen and Madlen took shelter in the chapel until they were chased away by a verger, and then they wandered the nearby streets, peering into shop windows, and trying as best they could to keep warm.

Later, as it was getting dark, they bought two more mutton pies from a seller on a street corner, holding the bags in their hands, the warm pies keeping out the chill, if only for a short while.

"Where will we sleep tonight?" Madlen asked, and Gwen shook her head.

"I don't know, Madlen. I'm sorry… perhaps we shouldn't have come here," she said, for it seemed there was no possibility of finding shelter, not that night, or perhaps ever…

Gwen feared the thought of having to return home, of what would happen to them when Reverend Llewelyn was forced to send them to the poorhouse or the orphanage. It made her shudder to think of it.

"But if we'd stayed, we'd have…" Madlen said, and Gwen nodded.

"I know… let's just wait and see what Bryn says when we see him later," Gwen replied, and so they waited until a distant church clock struck seven.

"Let's find Saint James' Place. Bryn said it wasn't far from the chapel," Gwen said.

They asked the pie seller for directions, and he pointed them along the street, telling them to turn left, then right, then right again.

"But if it's begging at the door you intend, be careful. You'll find yourself on the wrong side of the law," he said, tutting and shaking his head.

"We're not beggars," Gwen replied, even as she knew they were little more than street urchins in the vastness of the metropolis…

Saint James' Place was a handsome square, with a garden at its centre, bordered by iron railings. The town houses stood on three sides, with a street leading off where individual dwellings stood in their own gardens.

"Which one's the song school?" Madlen said, and together, they walked the length of the square, peering up at each house as they went.

Some of the windows were lit by lamps, but one house stood out, all its windows lit, and as they approached, Gwen gave a sigh of relief. A plaque next to the door declared it to be the song school, and steps led down to what appeared to be a servant's and tradesman's entrance below.

The clocks had not yet struck eight, and Gwen and Madlen waited outside, hoping they would not be caught or sent away. Eventually, the chimes across the city rang out, and the two of them stepped cautiously down the steps to the lower door.

Above, they could hear the distant sound of a solitary voice practising a melody, accompanied by a piano, carrying on the still night air as though coming from heaven itself.

"Isn't it beautiful?" Gwen said, imagining it might even be Bryn himself.

But a moment later, a bolt was slid back, and the door opened, revealing Bryn holding a candle. He ushered them inside, closing the door behind them, and they found themselves in a narrow passageway with storerooms leading off on either side.

"The servants have gone to bed. They have Sunday evenings off. We'll be safe. No one else comes down here at night. You must both be hungry," he said, and he led them into a large larder, where all manner of good things to eat–the remnants of a fine dinner, by the looks of it–stood on the shelves.

"We're very hungry," Gwen said, for the two

mutton pies had done little to suffice against the cold.

Bryn encouraged them to help themselves, and when they had eaten their fill, he took them along the corridor to a parlour that belonging to the cook. The remnants of a fire burned in the hearth.

"Now, I want to know everything," he said, turning to Gwen, who nodded.

"It was Reverend Llewlyn's doing," she said, and now she recounted the story of their extraordinary journey to London.

She left no detail unspoken, explaining how she and Madlen had been forced to flee after the arrival of the milk inspectors.

"And your uncle fled?" Bryn said, shaking his head in astonishment.

"And we don't know where he's gone, or what he's done with Owain, either," Madlen replied.

"They'd have charged him with murder, I'm certain of it," Gwen said, and Bryn shook his head.

"It's terrible, but we always knew there was the risk of it, didn't we? They couldn't carry on adulterating the milk—poisoning it—without someone discovering the truth eventually," he said.

"But we had to get away. Reverend Llewelyn would've sent us to the poorhouse or the orphanage. I know he would've done," Gwen said, and Bryn sighed.

"I know… and I'm so glad to see you, but… what are you going to do?" he asked.

Gwen blushed. It was the same question she had asked herself, and one she did not have a ready answer for. She had imagined Bryn might be the one to answer it, a solution presenting itself simply by virtue of their finding themselves in his company. But it had been foolish to think in such a way.

Bryn could surely do no more for them than they could do for themselves, and Gwen felt suddenly hopeless, fearing their only choice would be to return to Wales and the inevitable fate awaiting them.

"We… well, that's why we came to you. We don't know anyone else in London," Gwen said, and Bryn sighed.

"I… well, I can try to help you, but I don't know anyone, either. I've only been here a few weeks. We don't leave the song school much. Only to go to the chapel. There's the minister there, but… well, he might send you back to Reverend Llewlyn. Why did you tell him about your uncle and the milk? Didn't you know what would happen? He told me I'd have faced the same fate if it wasn't for my voice. He means well, of course, but there's nothing else he can do but send orphans to the orphanage and the older ones to the poorhouse. But here… if they catch you on the street, they may well do the same," he said, shaking his head sadly.

"But we need somewhere to stay tonight," Madlen said.

"You can stay here tonight. The servants won't come down until six O'clock, I don't think. Their bedrooms are above the dormitories, and I can hear them first thing in the morning. Sleep in one of the storerooms and slip out early. I'm sure I can manage to bring you food again tomorrow night, but I can't keep doing it. Someone's bound to get suspicious," he said, and Gwen nodded.

She was grateful to him for what he had done for them, and she knew it was a risk for him to continue helping them. They would sleep in one of the storerooms that night, but it seemed their only hope was to implore on the minister's charity, even if it meant what Gwen feared more than anything.

"Perhaps... we could get work somewhere as maids in a house?" she said, and Bryn nodded.

"I'm sure you could. But stay here tonight. I'll try to think of something, I promise. I'll see you tomorrow – we have prayers at nine. I'm supposed to be doing prep work now," he said, and Gwen smiled.

"I thought you sang beautifully this morning," she said, and he blushed.

THE MILK MAID ORPHAN

"You heard us then?" he asked, grinning at her, and Gwen nodded.

"We were at the back. I kept looking at you, but you were too busy concentrating on…" she said, and Bryna laughed as he interrupted her.

"The choirmaster," he said, and Gwen smiled.

"You're certainly made to work hard, aren't you?" she said, and he nodded.

"We're here to work. I'd be in the poorhouse if I wasn't here. I'm grateful to Reverend Llewlyn for sending me here, though it's taking some getting used to," he replied.

"I'm glad you're happy," Gwen said, and he smiled.

"I am, and you will be, too, both of you, I promise. But you should get some rest now. Try to sleep, and I'll see you tomorrow. Slip out early before the servants come down. You'll be quite alright," he said, and Gwen nodded.

She wanted to put her arms around him, to embrace him as she had done the last time she had seen him. But it felt strange to do so, as though there was a difference between them now, and instead, they simply said goodnight to one another before Bryn left them alone.

"What happens in the morning, Gwen?" Madlen asked.

She was forever asking questions, but Gwen

knew she was anxious. Everything was new – to them both – and Gwen shook her head, not knowing what the morning would bring.

"I don't know. But we'll have to leave early. Perhaps we could knock on the doors of some of the big houses hereabouts. We're bound to find someone looking for maids or even pot washers for the kitchens," she said.

In one of the storerooms, they found some bales of hay–for the hens Bryn had told them were kept in the garden–and with some rearranging, they were able to fashion a bed of sorts. They were both exhausted, having hardly slept at all the previous night, save for on the hard boards of the third-class compartment.

"I'll wake you up first thing in the morning," Gwen said, as the two sisters laid down next to one another, pulling their shawls around them for warmth.

"We're lucky to have Bryn, Gwen," Madlen said, and Gwen slipped her hand into her sister's and squeezed it.

"We certainly are," she replied, even as she knew they would still have to make their own way, come what may.

* * *

"Betty? Fetch the milk if it's arrived. I want to scald it before breakfast," a voice called out, and Gwen opened her eyes, confused for a moment as to where she was.

With a sudden jolt, she remembered, sitting bolt upright as the sound of footsteps in the corridor struck fear into her heart.

"They've not been yet, Mrs. Brooks. They're getting later every day," the voice of the one addressed as Betty replied.

Gwen shook Madlen awake, and her sister looked up at her through bleary eyes.

"What's wrong, Gwen? What is it?" she asked.

"We've slept late. The servants are awake," Gwen hissed, and Madlen's eyes grew wide with fear.

Gwen took her by the hand. They would have to make a run for it and now they stood at the storeroom door, listening for any sounds coming from beyond.

"That dairy. They must've changed their round. We're always the last, and the boys drink so much milk. I'll be having words," a voice from along the corridor, presumably that of Mrs. Brooks, said.

Gwen opened the storeroom door cautiously and peered out. There was no one to be seen, though the sound of voices could still be heard from the far end of the passageway. They would have to make a run for it, and together, Gwen and Madlen hurried towards the door leading to the outside. There was a bolt across it, and Gwen cut her hand in her haste to pull it back, the door creaking loudly as she pulled it open.

"You didn't close the door, Betty. There's a draught," Mrs. Brooks shouted, but before they could be discovered, Gwen and Madlen had hurried out of the door, slamming it behind them.

They hurried up the steps, crossing the square to the gardens, breathless from the exertion of their escape.

"Do you think anyone saw us?" Madlen asked, but Gwen shook her head.

"No, we weren't seen," she said, glancing back towards the song school.

She pictured Bryn eating his breakfast and wondered when they would next see him. She had thought the matter of coming to London would be a simple one, but it was proving far from so. Her whole body ached from the night spent sleeping on the hay bales and from the cold.

"What do we do now?" Madlen asked, but Gwen shook her head.

"Well, we've still got some money. We can buy something to eat, and then we could try knocking on some of the doors hereabouts, looking for work," she said.

But as she spoke, Gwen's attention was caught by

the sight of a cart approaching along the street. It was pulled by two large horses, and had a covered top, with the words *"Jones & Company, dairy and milk delivery"* on the side.

This was the expected delivery, and a young boy, no older than Madlen, now jumped from the front board to carry a churn of milk down the steps to the song school.

"A dairy," Madlen said, and Gwen nodded.

"Yes, a dairy... I wonder..." she replied, a sudden thought occurring to her, and taking her sister's hand, she stepped forward to approach the driver, who looked down at her and nodded.

"Good morning, miss," he said.

It was the first friendly word, apart from that of Bryn, they had heard since arriving in London. Gwen smiled at him.

"Excuse me, are you Jones?" she asked, and the man laughed.

"No, I'm "company." Harry Bartlett at your service," he said, leaning down and offering Gwen his hand.

The boy had now returned with an empty milk churn, the sound of Betty's chastisements following him up the steps of the song school.

"And I want a quart of cream tomorrow, and don't you be late," she called out.

The boy rolled his eyes, glancing at Gwen and smiling.

"A quart of cream for the song school," he said, and Harry nodded.

"We'll do the round backwards tomorrow. She can have her cream at dawn, and the pleasure of being woken up to it," he said, laughing and shaking his head.

"Please… we've just arrived in London, from Wales. We lived with our uncle, but… well, we had to leave. It was a dairy farm. I was a milkmaid, and a lot of other things beside it. Do you… might you… have a job for me? And for my sister, too?" Gwen asked.

Harry Bartlett scratched his head and smiled.

"Well… it's funny you should say that. We do need a milkmaid, as it turns out. That's why we're late on the round. We don't have enough time to see to the herd and be ready on time for the deliveries. It's a small herd, mind you. We used to buy milk from the Welsh farms and sell it on, but it's not what it used to be…" he said, shaking his head.

"We know how to milk cows," Madlen said, and Harry nodded.

"We could only pay one of you. But there's a place for you to sleep, and you could share our meals with us. That's what Joe here does. Alright… I'll give you a trial. The dairy's not far from here. Climb in," he said, nodding to the back of the cart.

Gwen and Madlen looked at one another and smiled. It was an answer to prayer, and just the good fortune they needed. They climbed onto the back of the cart, their legs dangling down, and Harry clicked off the horses.

"We did it, Gwen," Madlen whispered, slipping her hand into Gwen's, and Gwen could only hope her sister was right.

PART III

JONES & COMPANY

London, Winter, 1866

Gwen was now eighteen years old, and she and Madlen had worked for Harry Bartlett for six years at the dairy close to the song school. They lived in a small room above the milking parlour, and though their days were long and their duties onerous, life had treated them kindly. Certainly, more so than if they had remained in Wales.

Each morning, they rose early to bring the herd in from the barn, milking the cows, and filling the churns with the fresh milk for Harry and Joe to take on their deliveries. During the morning, they worked in the dairy, making cheese and butter to sell, but the afternoons were their own, and they would often go to the chapel to hear the choir from the song school rehearsing.

"They're giving Bryn a solo at the Christmas carol concert," Gwen said, as she and Madlen walked together through the snowy streets one December afternoon.

The winter that year had arrived with a bite, bringing with it heavy snow and ice, and some mornings, the milk in the buckets had frozen solid.

"They should give you a solo, too, Gwen," Madlen replied, and Gwen laughed.

She still loved to sing, and in the summer, when it was pleasant to be in the milking parlour at an early hour with the sun rising outside, she would sing to the cows. She still remembered all the old songs and hymns she had learned as a child, and it always delighted her to hear the choir from the song school rehearsing.

"They won't allow girls to sing in the choir. It's very different to what it was back in the valley," Gwen replied.

She had once asked the choirmaster if she might be allowed to join the boys for their rehearsals, and had even sung to him, much to his annoyance.

"Girls don't sing in a chapel choir," he had told her, and that had been the end of the matter.

As they approached the chapel, the sound of the rehearsal echoed out onto the street. They were practising Christmas carols, and the familiar words to *Hark the Herald Angels Sing* could be heard as they made their way up the steps to the chapel door. The minister, Reverend Aethon Brynmoor, knew them well, and he nodded to them as they slipped into a pew at the back of the chapel.

"Look, we're just in time to hear Bryn's solo," Madlen whispered, as Bryn now stepped forward.

"Hail the heaven-born Prince of Peace!
Hail the Sun of Righteousness!
Light and life to all He brings
Risen with healing in His wings
Mild He lays His glory by
Born that man no more may die
Born to raise the sons of earth
Born to give them second birth
Hark! The herald angels sing
"Glory to the new-born king.""

THE REST of the choir now took up the third and final verse, but Gwen could not take her eyes off Bryn, who now stepped back into his place with the rest. He had the voice of an angel, or so it seemed, and had proved himself entirely worthy of Reverend Llewlyn's trust in him.

This was to be his final year at the song school, and as for what happened next, Bryn did not know. He hoped to stay in London and make a living from singing–perhaps in a chorus or at one of the theatres.

Gwen, too, was wondering about her future, and that of Madlen, too. They could not remain as milkmaids forever, as kind and generous as Harry Bartlett had been to them.

"Right, thank you, boys and men. We'll take a break now, only for a few moments, mind you," the choirmaster, Mr. Jones, said.

He was the same Jones as Gwen's employer, the two of them being brothers who had come to London from the Welsh valleys in their younger days. But Mr. Jones, the dairy owner, was often away on business, and it was Harry Bartlett who ran the dairy in his absence.

Mr. Jones, the choirmaster, was a formidable man, but the choir was highly respected, and the carol concert would draw large crowds. Bryn now came hurrying up the aisle to greet them, smiling, as Gwen and Madlen rose to their feet.

"Did you hear the solo?" he asked, and Gwen nodded.

"You were wonderful," she said, and Bryn blushed.

"I don't think I hit the top notes, and my finishes weren't crisp enough. I still need to practice a great deal," he said.

To Gwen's untrained ear he had sounded perfect, but Bryn always set himself to the highest standards, and she knew he would not be happy until every note was as he believed it should be.

"It sounded perfect," Madlen said, but Bryn shook his head.

"Not yet and Mr. Jones won't be happy until it is," he said.

Gwen smiled at him. She loved to hear him sing, and the two of them still sang together whenever they had the opportunity. Sometimes, Bryn would come to the dairy, and the two of them would sing together as Gwen churned the milk for the butter. He would tell her how good she was, even as Gwen herself always thought her voice sounded flat.

"It's a beautiful carol," Gwen said, and Bryn smiled.

"Christmas carols are my favourite things to sing," he said.

"We'll be at the concert. We've both been looking forward to it," Gwen said.

"I'm glad, but I've got something to tell you. I received a letter from Reverend Llewlyn. He writes to me occasionally. He thinks I'll be returning to the valley to lead the chapel choir to new heights of glory. But had some interesting things to say in his latest letter," Bryn said, reaching into his pocket and pulling out an envelope.

Gwen was curious to know what the minister had to say. She had no contact with anyone in the valley, and neither she nor Madlen had returned there since the day they had left on the milk train.

She knew Bryn and Reverend Llewlyn maintained a correspondence, but Gwen herself had always been wary of contacting the minister lest he should have reason to want to know where she was.

She knew nothing of what had become of her uncle, of Cadell, or of Owain. The past was another country, and her memories of it were clouded.

"What did he say?" she asked, as Bryn unfolded the letter.

"He writes to say your uncle's farm remains untenanted and there was never a definite claim by the milk board. They just shut it down. No one knows anything about where your uncle went or what happened to him. He asked me about you, too," Bryn said.

"About me? But why now? It's been six years since we left," Gwen said, fearing the possibility of her and Madlen being sought to blame for the adulteration of the milk, even after all these years.

"It seems your name was mentioned in passing, and he was curious to know what happened to you. I've never mentioned him to you. He doesn't know you're here. But it's interesting to think your uncle's farm is still vacant. He also writes to say there have been some cases of adulterated milk in the valley, though no one knows the source. It's all very odd, isn't it?" Bryn said, folding up the letter and replacing it in his pocket.

"It is, yes," Gwen replied, shuddering at the thought of what might have been.

She did not have the slightest inclination as to what had become of her uncle and the others. They had simply disappeared, along with any chance of bringing them to justice for their crimes.

Since arriving in London, Gwen had learned of many cases involving the adulteration of milk. The practice was widespread, as it was with bread, too. Chalk would be added to dough, just as it was to milk, along with various other unpleasant substances, some of which had proved lethal. At least a dozen deaths had been linked to adulterated milk, and there was no doubt in Gwen's mind as there being many more, too.

"I wouldn't dream of adding anything to the milk. It's a wicked practice. Milk is milk. That's all," Harry Bartlett often said, and Gwen was glad to work for a man so scrupulous in his morals.

"But do you think it could be my uncle? The adulterated milk, I mean," Gwen said, but Bryn shook his head.

"Not after all this time. But I've heard rumours of the same in London, too. It's a terrible crime. People are getting sick–it's like the water pumps," he said, shaking his head.

"Alright, boys and men. Take your places again, please. We'll start with *Silent Night*," Mr. Jones called out, and Bryn nodded to them.

"I'll see you later. I could come to the dairy after I've finished rehearsing," he said, and Gwen smiled.

"I'd like that," she said, and he smiled back at her, before hurrying back down the aisle to take his place with the others.

Gwen watched him go, her thoughts on Reverend Llewlyn's letter. It was curious to think of her uncle's farm still vacant, and to know the practice of adulterating the milk continued. She had not thought about her uncle or the others for some time, preferring to forget her ordeal at their hands.

Now, as she and Madlen walked back to the dairy, she could not help but wonder what had become of them.

"Owain will be all grown up now," she said, and Madlen nodded.

"And no doubt still as horrible as he was before," she replied.

"I hope… perhaps you're right," Gwen replied, for though it pained her to think of her brother involved with such things, the choice had been his.

"They're welcome to one another," Madlen said, and Gwen sighed.

"I think you're right," she replied, but as they returned to the dairy, Gwen's thoughts were distracted by speculations as to what her brother's fate had been, and she was curious to know what had happened to him, to her uncle, and to her cousin.

"Perhaps they're still doing the same as they were before," she thought to herself, for it would not have surprised her to know her uncle was still involved in the abhorrent practice of adulterating the milk.

"I don't want to see any of them ever again," Madlen said, and Gwen nodded.

"Well, you won't have to," she replied, hoping her words were true.

THE SURPRISE INSPECTION

Gwen sat on the milking stool, bleary-eyed, and still half asleep. It was cold in the milking parlour, and the milk in the buckets was already growing icy. Madlen was sitting behind her, the two having almost finished milking the small herd they had brought in from the barn an hour or so before. It was still dark outside, and the milking parlour was lit by a lamp hanging from the ceiling.

"We'll fill the last bucket, then fill the churns," Gwen said, turning to her sister, who nodded.

"We need to keep two back for the butter, Harry said we need ten pats today," Madlen replied.

"We should have enough. Goodness me, I can hardly keep my eyes open today. I'm so tired and cold," she said.

"I hope you're not coming down with anything," Madlen said, and Gwen pulled her shawl tightly around her shoulders.

"No… I don't think so. I'm just tired, and it's so cold in here," she said, and Madlen nodded.

"It certainly is. Come on, let's finish the milking, then we can take the buckets into Lisette," she said.

Lisette was the other milk maid, a fiery-tempered girl of sixteen, with red hair and bright blue eyes. She could be temperamental, but she had a good heart, and a kindness about her, too.

The two sisters got on well with her and had been encouraging her to come to the chapel with them to hear Bryn sing. Lisette was an orphan, and Harry Bartlett had taken pity on her in much the same way as he had with Gwen and Madlen.

"That's the last of the buckets," Gwen said as she and Madlen brought them into the dairy where Lisette was measuring the milk into churns.

"And I've just finished the last of these. We'll be ready to load the cart up shortly. I've not seen Harry this morning. Should we go and wake him up?" she said, with a mischievous look in her eyes.

Gwen smiled. Harry lived in a small cottage attached to the dairy. He often slept late, but at that moment, the sound of voices in the yard outside caused the three of them to look up in surprise. It was still early, not yet light, but lamplight now appeared through the windows, and the sound of Harry's voice called out across the yard.

"Who's there? What's all this?" he shouted.

"Milk board. We're inspecting the dairy," came the reply, and the door of the dairy now opened, revealing several men holding lamps.

"You'll not find anything wrong here," Lisette exclaimed, folding her arms and facing the men with a defiant glare.

One of them smiled.

"It's alright, miss. If there's nothing untoward, then there's no problem. But we've had a lot of reports of milk being adulterated lately. We don't know the source. That's why we're checking all the dairies in the city," he said, as the other men now began to make their inspection.

Harry appeared behind them, and Gwen, Madlen, and Lisette could do nothing more than step back and allow the men to conduct their inspections. They made a thorough search of dairy, checking the stores and examining the milking parlour.

Gwen knew there was nothing for them to find. The dairy was spotless, and the milk was as fresh as it could be. In the six years she had worked for Jones & Company, there had never been any suggestion of adulterating the milk, and Gwen knew Harry abhorred such practices.

"Milk is milk," he would say, and that was the end of the matter.

But despite knowing this, Gwen could not help but fear the milk inspectors, recalling their similar search of her uncle's farm. When that had occurred, Gwen had found herself homeless and forced to flee, and the memories of that fateful night were forever imprinted on in her mind.

"There's nothing here. No problems, Mr. Bartlett," the lead inspector said after the men had finished their work.

"We could've told you that," Lisette said, shaking her head.

The inspector smiled.

"I'm sure you could. But we had to be sure. I want to impress on you the seriousness of this. There have been deaths. Poisoned milk was the cause. Someone's responsible for it. We thought we'd eradicated this problem, but it seems we haven't. If you hear anything or if anyone tries to sell you chalk or other additives, report it. And if anyone tries to sell you milk, be sure to check it for yourselves," he said, and Harry nodded.

"We will, but we're already late with the deliveries this morning. Are we free to go?" he asked, and the inspector nodded.

"Yes, we've seen everything we need to see.

Thank you for your cooperation," he said, and nodding to them, he left, followed by the others.

Harry breathed a sigh of relief.

"I wasn't expecting that," he said.

"Well, they weren't going to find anything, were they?" Lisette replied.

"We once had an inspection on my uncle's farm," Gwen said.

She had not told Harry or Lisette the full story about her uncle and the adulterated milk. It shamed her to think of it, even as she had come to realise there was nothing she could have done to prevent it.

"What happened?" Harry asked, and Gwen now recounted, as best she could, the story of her uncle and the adulterated milk.

Harry and Lisette listened, and Harry shook his head as her story came to a conclusion.

"We had to leave. We'd have been sent to the poorhouse or the orphanage if we hadn't," Gwen said, and Harry nodded.

"It's a wicked practice. People are dying. It's no wonder the inspectors are coming down hard on the dairies. I'm only grateful… well, it's tempting, I suppose. The milk doesn't fetch a fair price, and there're those who would adulterate it for their own gains. Watering it down does no harm to it though I wouldn't do it myself. But as for adding chalk, and whatever else goes into it…" he said, shaking his head.

"I still don't know what happened to my uncle and the others. They escaped, but where to, I don't know," Gwen said.

"Perhaps they came to London. There's no shortage of work here, and they might easily have got jobs in one of the dairies or abattoirs," Harry said.

It made Gwen nervous to think her uncle and cousin might be close by, even as she had no reason to think it or to be suspicious of the possibility. She and Madlen kept themselves to themselves. They rarely went further than the chapel or the song school, and had few friends, save for Bryn and Lisette.

"Perhaps, or they might've gone north," Madlen said.

"To Manchester or Newcastle, even. Yes, that's the thing about milk, everyone needs it," Harry said.

"Hadn't we better get on with making the deliveries?" Lisette said, and Harry nodded.

"You're right. We're already running late. I can just hear Mrs. Brooks at the song school shouting at me. Come along, let's get the cart loaded, then we can be off," he said, and the four of them set to work, loading the cart with the churns.

The sun had risen by the time the delivery had

set off, and Gwen and Madlen watched from the milking parlour door as the cart was driven out of the yard, the sound of the horses' hooves clip-clopping on the cobbles.

"Do you think it's Uncle Dawid?" Madlen asked, as they returned to the dairy to begin making the butter.

Gwen shook her head.

"I don't think so, no. Why would it be? Anyone can adulterate milk, can't they? It's just a matter of adding whatever unpleasant extra one chooses. No, they're long gone, Gwen. It would be too risky for them to do it again. They got away with it once, but they wouldn't get away with it again," she replied.

She wanted to believe her own words, even as she feared her uncle and cousin *would* be willing to take such a risk. Cadell had been blasé about his work, boasting of it, even to the day of the arrival of the milk inspectors.

He had been willing to take a terrible risk for profit, and Gwen could not imagine he had changed. She was worried about Owain, too. She often thought of her brother, and how easily he had been led astray.

"And if we did see them again?" Madlen asked.

"Let's not think about it, Madlen. We've got butter to make," Gwen replied, and the two sisters now began the laborious process of churning the milk to separate the curds.

But in the coming days, Gwen could not help but continue to think about her uncle, and the possibility of where these new and dangerous batches of milk were coming from…

* * *

Christmas was fast approaching, and there was a great deal of excitement at the prospect of the coming concert given by the choir from the song school. Gwen and Madlen sat through all the rehearsals, and despite Bryn's claims to the contrary, there was no doubting his solo performance was to be the crowning glory.

"I think I know all the carols by heart," Madlen said as they waited for Bryn at the door of the chapel.

He emerged with several of the other boys, but held back, smiling as Gwen and Madlen approached.

"I heard about the inspection," he said.

"They're inspecting all the dairies in this part of the city and further afield, too. It was a complete surprise. They didn't find anything, of course, but the inspector said there's a lot of adulterated milk around now. They just don't know the source," Gwen replied.

"And so, they check the dairies least likely to be involved. It won't be an established business like yours. It'll be one of the back street dairies, like the abattoirs," Bryn said.

He was right, of course. Harry had said the same. Milk was supplied from across the city, taken to cooperatives and distributed. Anyone could sell milk, and despite the inspections, there would be many small producers who were not checked.

"You're right. But it doesn't mean they don't have to check," Gwen replied.

"It's just like Reverend Llewelyn said, isn't it? The same thing repeating itself again," Bryan said, shaking his head.

"I can still taste it, the adulterated milk, I mean. I tried it once. The chalk makes it thick and creamy, but it's cloying, too, and leave the most unpleasant feeling in the mouth. I'd know it an instant if I tried it again," Gwen said, for she had unpleasant memories of trying the milk in the dairy at her uncle's farm after Cadell had added the chalk to it.

"But once it's mixed into other things, I doubt anyone would know it," Bryn said.

"It's nothing to do with my uncle, though. He's long gone, and Cadell and Owain, too," Gwen said, for she was still trying to convince herself the matter had nothing to do with her or her past.

Bryn nodded.

"I think you're right. They'd be fools to try anything. Utter fools," he replied.

"Don't let us hold you up. We'll see you at the concert," Gwen said, smiling, as Bryn hurried off after the other choir boys.

"He always smiles at you a certain way," Madlen said, and Gwen blushed.

"What do you mean?" she replied, and her sister raised her eyebrows.

"You know very well what I mean, Gwen. When he looks at you, it's not like he looks at me or anyone else. He has a certain way of smiling. I can't describe it exactly, but he does. And so do you. The way you look at him…" she said.

Gwen shook her head. She did not think Bryn smiled at her any differently to the way he smiled at anyone else. She did not think so, at least. But as for the way she looked at him…

"Well, perhaps I do smile at him a certain way. I just… it's the way I've always looked at him. We've known him for so long, and we've been through so much together," Gwen replied.

But her sister was right. Her feelings for Bryn had grown stronger recently. It was confusing, and she did not fully understand how she felt. She had always loved him. He was like family to her, but now there was something else, too.

Gwen did not know how Bryn felt about her, but

there was no doubting the obvious affection between them. But Gwen was worried, too. Bryn's time at the song school was ending, and she did not know where he would go or what he would do when his time there was over.

They had not discussed it, even as it loomed large in her thoughts. She did not want to think about it, and yet it was playing on her mind.

"Yes… but the two of you… it's different. I know you'll miss him terribly if he has to leave. Will we stay?" Madlen asked.

Gwen shook her head. She did not know the answer, as much for herself as for her sister. They had nowhere else to go, and Harry Bartlett had been unfailingly kind in allowing them to remain at the dairy, giving them work and their board.

If Bryn was to leave the song school, there would be nothing to keep them in London, and recently, Gwen had been longing for the pure air and open vistas of the Welsh valleys.

London was dirty, its streets choked with smog, and there were days when it sank Gwen into a deep depression. She had always wanted to see it, but her years of being forced to reside there were taking their toll.

If Bryn was to leave, Gwen knew she would want to leave with him…

"I don't know. I don't want to think about it,

Madlen. It upsets me," Gwen said, taking a deep breath.

Her sister slipped her arm into Madlen's, the two of them walking back towards the dairy. Snow was beginning to fall, and there was a chill in the air. It was cold, and Gwen was looking forward to hot muffins spread with the butter they had made that morning.

"I'm sure we'll find a way. We always we, don't we?" she said, and Gwen nodded.

"We seem to, but I just can't stop thinking about Uncle Dawid and the others. All this business with the adulterated milk. Do you think… I know it's impossible, but… I just can't help wondering where they are. It all seems so strange," Gwen said, shaking her head.

"I feel the same but it's just the memory of it all, Gwen. They're long gone," Madlen replied, and Gwen could only hope her sister was speaking the truth…

A DISTURBING SIGHT

"I want to welcome all of you, friends, and benefactors, from near and far, to the concert this evening. As you know, it's given by the choir of the song school, and intended to raise funds for the orphanage on Benwell Street. We're glad to have the governors with us. Gentleman, you're very welcome. Our concert begins with that well-known carol *It Came upon the Midnight Clear*," the minister said, before stepping to one side as the song school choir came forward.

The chapel was packed, and Gwen and Madlen had been forced to sit near the back. Gwen hoped Bryn would see them, and now she smiled at the sight of him at the front of the choir as the carol began.

The choir sang beautifully, and with the chapel lit

by candlelight and filled with the praises of the holy infant, Gwen was caught up in the mystery and beauty of Christmas.

"It's nearly time for Bryn's solo, I think," Madlen whispered.

The choir had sung several carols, and there had been readings from scripture, and a poem about the tradition of the yule log. The choirmaster now beckoned Bryn forward, and Gwen strained her neck to see.

If he was nervous, it did not show, and now he glanced towards the organist and nodded. The organ struck up gently and Bryn began to sing.

"Silent night! Holy night!
All is calm, all is bright
Round yon virgin mother and child!
Holy infant, so tender and mild,
Sleep in heavenly peace!
Sleep in heavenly peace!

Silent night! Holy night!
Shepherds quake at the sight!
Glories stream from heaven afar,
Heavenly hosts sing Alleluia!

Christ the Saviour is born!
Christ the Saviour is born!

Silent night! Holy night!
Son of God, love's pure light
Radiant beams from thy holy face
With the dawn of redeeming grace,
Jesus, Lord, at thy birth!
Jesus, Lord, at thy birth!"

THE CHAPEL WAS as silent as the night the carol sang of. Bryn sang exquisitely, and there was not a single note out of place. Gwen had tears in her eyes when the solo concluded, and she slipped her hand into Madlen's, squeezing it, and glancing at her sister, who smiled.

"It reminds me of home," she whispered, for the image of the stable was just as she imagined the farm, and despite all the troubles she had endured there, she missed the place terribly, if not the people.

"Me, too. It was beautiful," Madlen replied.

The concert continued, but Gwen could think of little else but Bryn's performance. It had been remarkable, and she could not wait to congratulate him.

The choir sang a repertoire of carols, and at the end, the audience was encouraged to join in with a rendition of *God Rest ye Merry Gentlemen*, sung with much gusto. Afterwards, collection plates were passed along the pews, and a generous amount was given to support the orphanage.

There was to be a reception in the vestry afterwards, but only the choir and certain members of the audience were invited.

"I don't think we'll be able to see Bryn after all. We'll see him tomorrow," Gwen said, watching as the choir filed off the stage.

Bryn turned, glancing out across the pews, and he caught Gwen's eyes, smiling at her as she smiled back.

"You're doing it again, Gwen," Madlen said, and Gwen blushed.

"I just want him to know how proud I am of him," Gwen replied.

"I'm sure he knows. We'll see him tomorrow. But come along, they'll be turning down the gas lamps shortly, and it'll get cold in here," Madlen said.

The rest of the audience, those not invited to the reception, were filing out, calling out Christmas greetings to one another. Gwen and Madlen followed, standing on the steps of the chapel, and looking up at the starry sky above.

The moon was nearly full, casting a silvery light over the city, and Gwen pulled her shawl tightly around her shoulders against the cold.

"It's going to be a frosty night. It might snow again, too," she said, and Madlen nodded.

"Yes, come on, we'll get back to the dairy, stoke up the fire and make toast with the toasting fork. I want to sit as close to the flames as possible. At least Harry's generous with the coal," she said, and Gwen laughed.

"We'll both sit close to it. Come along," she said.

The last of the audience were filing out of the chapel, and the street was busy. Hansom cabs were being hailed, whilst others set off walking this way and that. As Gwen and Madlen walked down the steps, a sudden and surprising sight caught Gwen's eyes.

Three men were walking past, pushing others out of their way as they did so, and causing a disturbance at the bottom of the steps.

"Get out of it, get out of the way," one of them said, and Gwen's heart skipped a beat.

The voice was unmistakable — it was her Uncle Dawid. Gwen seized Madlen's arm, pulling her back as the three men passed. Six years had passed since Gwen had last laid eyes on her uncle, and even in the moonlight, it was hard to tell if it was really him. But the voice was unmistakable.

"Madlen..." Gwen gasped, and the two of them clung to one another.

"But it can't be... it sounded just like..." Madlen said, and Gwen nodded.

"Like Uncle Dawid and look, three of them," she said, and they watched as the three men walked on along the street.

Gwen had not been able to see any of them properly, but she felt certain it was them. Owain would be much taller now–almost a man, and Cadell, too, would have grown more into the likeness of his father.

"It has to be them, Madlen... at least, we need to be sure," Gwen said, recovering herself from the shock.

She wondered if her uncle had come to look for them, or whether it was simply the strangest of coincidences. Her thoughts returned to the adulterated milk, and her heart skipped a beat, fearing her suspicions were realised.

"We could follow them," Madlen said, and Gwen nodded.

She knew it was dangerous, but she had to be certain. The street was lit by gas lamps, and stretched along a row of terraced houses, with a small park opposite and the chapel standing at one end.

If they did not hurry, they would easily lose the three men in the maze of streets, and now they, too, pushed through the crowd, trying to keep the three men in sight.

"They're heading towards Saint James' Place and the song school. Do you think they know Bryn lives there?" Madlen said, as they followed the men on through the streets.

"I doubt it. The more I think about it, the less likely it seems they know anything. Why would they risk exposing themselves? Surely, they know they're still wanted men," Gwen replied.

Her uncle had become a wicked man, but he was no fool. She could only imagine he and the others had come to London for means of business, or some other nefarious scheme. They could surely have no suspicion Gwen and Madlen were there.

No one else knew of their escape to London six years ago, except the stationmaster, and even then, a great deal of time had passed. They could be anywhere, and it seemed fate was responsible for bringing them together once again.

"They're fools to come here. I don't understand it," Madlen replied.

"It'll be for some financial gain, I'm certain of it," Gwen said.

The men now turned into Saint James' Place, but they walked straight past the song school, oblivious, or so it seemed, to their own connections there. It was another half a mile, turning this way and that, before they stopped.

There was no one else around, and the trail had led to an insalubrious part of the city, where narrows alleys and dark warehouses concealed an underbelly of crime and unsavoury goings on.

"I don't like it," Madlen whispered.

"Stay in the shadows," Gwen replied, desperate to get closer and overhear something of what the three men were saying to one another.

She did not know exactly where they were–a street like so many others in that part of the city, with the backs of tenements rising above them, dark and foreboding. There were no gas lamps here, and a faint smog was hanging in the air.

"Be careful," Madlen whispered, as they edged a little closer.

"I'm telling you, Cadell, it's not the right time. They're already suspicious. Don't be so impatient. If we bide our time…" Gwen's uncle was saying, but he was interrupted by Cadell, whose unmistakable voice now echoed through the shadows.

"I'm done biding my time. We don't have time. The profits are there for the taking, and if it's not us who takes them, it'll be someone else. Now, do we, or don't we? Owain agrees with me, don't you, Owain?" he snarled.

"I… I do," Owain replied, and Gwen's heart sank to hear her brother speak.

He sounded forlorn, as though reluctant to agree, even as it seemed he had no choice but to do so.

"There, you see, Father? It's agreed. We'll finish the job we started with no delays," Cadell said.

The men now walked on, turning into a yard through an arch. A lamp was burning above it, and through the gloom, Gwen could just about make out the words on the board, the peeling paint having faded to just an outline.

"*Robinson's Dairy,*" she read, whispering the words to Madlen, even as she dared not get any closer.

"It's terrible," Madlen whispered.

There was no doubt in Gwen's mind as to what was happening. Her uncle and cousin had not changed, and, having lain low for the past six years, they were back. The operation would be just the same, adulterating the milk and flooding the market with it to make as much profit as possible.

Her uncle would not care what harm it did–his only concern would be the profit he made from the sales. But it seemed it was Cadell who was the driving force behind this renewed wickedness, and he would allow nothing, not even his own father, to get in the way of his own lust for fortune.

"Come along, we need to find Bryn and tell him," Gwen said, for she knew he would want to know what they had discovered, and taking her sister's hand, the two of them hurried back through the dark streets towards the song school.

* * *

"I THOUGHT we'd heard the last of them. I prayed we'd heard the last of them," Bryn said, shaking his head.

Gwen and Madlen had arrived back at the song school just as the choir was returning from the reception, and Bryn had invited them in out of the cold. Gwen and Madlen were now well known by the rest of the choir and by the choirmaster. Now they stood in the hallway with Bryn, having explained to him everything they had seen.

"I hoped so, too, but it *was* them. There's no doubt about it," Gwen replied.

Any sense of festive cheer was gone. She was worried, even as she felt certain her uncle's arrival in the capital so close to the dairy and the song school was a coincidence. But seeing him again and Cadell and Owain had brought back unpleasant memories, and Gwen could not help but fear what might happen if her uncle, or one of the others, was to learn she and Madlen were nearby.

"And what about the milk? What can we do to stop them?" Bryn said.

Gwen was certain the milk the inspectors from the milk board had spoken about had been adulterated by her uncle and cousin. That, or they hoped to undercut the market by doing the same. Back in the valley, adulterated milk had often come from different farms, and competition had existed between them.

It would be just the same in the capital, but as for what to do about it, Gwen was uncertain. She had no evidence her uncle and cousin had committed a crime, only a near certain suspicion they were doing so.

It made her angry to think of it, and she felt determined to do something about it. To inform the milk board would only result in the milk being hurriedly poured away. Gwen had no doubt her uncle had learned from his previous mistakes, and she felt certain the inspectors would find nothing if they raided Robinson's Dairy.

"We must catch them in the act. Someone needs to report them and have evidence to prove their claim. We need some of the milk from the dairy. I'd know just what it tastes like," Gwen said, and Bryn nodded.

"But how do we get it? You can't exactly walk in

there and buy a churn for yourself, can you?" he said, and Gwen shook her head.

"No… I know I can't, but… well… we'll think of something. We've got to think of something, haven't we? Oh… it's too terrible for words," she exclaimed, and tears welled up in her eyes.

She had not meant to cry, and she felt foolish for doing so. But the sight of her uncle, her cousin and brother had brought back such terrible memories as to be quite overwhelming.

Gwen and Madlen had built a new and better life for themselves in London. They had left the past behind, and though there were times when Gwen longed for the valleys and the clear mountain air, she would not have swapped her current circumstances for the old. Her life was hard, but it was honest, and she was surrounded by good people. But this…

"It's alright. You're not in any danger, Gwen. They can't do anything to you. In fact, if they knew you were here, I think they'd be worried," Bryn said, and to Gwen's surprise and relief he put his arms around her.

Tears rolled down her cheeks, and she rested her head on his shoulder, clinging to him, sobbing as he held her close.

"I'm sorry," she gasped.

"You don't have to be sorry. I know the terrible things you suffered. It's not your fault, Gwen. You didn't ask to be involved in any of this. Cruel circumstances brought it about. The death of your aunt, the moral failings of your uncle… it's not your fault," he said, and Gwen nodded, looking up at him through tear-filled eyes.

"I know… I just… oh, it's too awful," she exclaimed.

"And we'll put a stop to it. But we must be certain first," Bryn said.

"Then we need a plan. We need to get some of the milk. We'd both know the taste, wouldn't we, Gwen?" Madlen said, and Gwen nodded.

She knew the taste all too well, a cloying, clinging, starchy taste. The chalk turned the milk creamy, with an attractive appearance, but the taste was foul. To drink it as it would make anyone sick, but when it was added to other ingredients–mixed into cakes or used in sauces–there was no telling. In this way, many people had fallen ill, and the source of the illness was difficult to discover.

"I'd know it immediately–and the way it feels in the mouth, too. But we must be careful. We must find a way of getting some of the milk before it's sent off and in such a way as to prove where it came from," Gwen replied.

She imagined her uncle and cousin would only be selling to wholesalers, making any trace on the milk nigh on impossible. Once the churns were bottled, the milk could go to any corner of the city, and that they sold to small producers, boarding houses, and restaurants, would find its way into the food being consumed by the unsuspecting customers who would never realise what it was they were suffering from when they fell ill.

"I'll try to think of something–somewhere from here could go, one of the choirboys, though I doubt they'd sell it to just anyone. No… you uncle's too clever for that, and he'll have learned from his mistakes, too, I'm certain of it," Bryn said.

Gwen sighed. She did not have the strength for any more that night. The sight of her uncle and cousin had struck fear into her heart, and the sight of her brother had brought back a sense of remorse over what had happened to him.

"I should've done more for Owain," Gwen said, as she and Madlen walked back to the dairy later that evening.

"But you couldn't have done any more for him, Gwen. He made his own bed," Madlen replied.

"But he was so young. He shouldn't have… I shouldn't have…" Gwen said, but Madlen shook her head.

"You did everything you could for him, Gwen. You were only young, too. We both were. I know it's not right, but… you don't know what he's like now. He was becoming more and more like Cadell every day. Don't you remember some of the things he said? He was cruel, and the more I think of him... well, I don't want him to be my brother," Madlen said.

But Gwen was thinking back to the way her brother had spoken when they had overheard him earlier than night. He had sounded reluctant, as though he was now regretting his involvement with their uncle and cousin.

As a child, Owain had been enamoured by Cadell, and their cousin had used this to his advantage, manipulating Owain and making him his own. But now, Owain had grown up, and Gwen could only hope he had changed. Perhaps he was questioning his loyalties, and she wondered if there was the possibility of using such a question against their uncle and cousin...

"But he is your brother, Madlen. There's no escaping from that. He deserves more than this. Don't you think?" Gwen asked.

"And what about us? Didn't we deserve more than what we got?" Madlen replied.

Gwen knew her sister was angry with their uncle, angry at the way they had been treated. She, too, wanted justice to be done, but to think of seeing Owain punished, too, filled her heart with sorrow.

"I know, but he was only a child," Gwen replied.

They had reached the dairy now, and they found

Lisette waiting for them at the door to the milking parlour, holding a lantern.

"Oh, thank goodness you're back. I thought something terrible had happened. Where have you both been?" she asked, and Gwen sighed.

"Come inside out of the cold. We'll explain everything," she said, and she ushered the two of them into the milking parlour.

But as she closed the door behind them, Gwen could not help shuddering at the thought of what had happened that evening, and drawing the bolt across the door, she could only hope her uncle and cousin would not find them, even as she knew the time to confront them was drawing near…

LISETTE'S ADVENTURE

"It's terrible, just like the milk inspectors said. I've not slept a wink thinking about it. But... I didn't think... and you're certain it was them?" Lisette asked, as she, Gwen, and Madlen worked in the dairy the next morning.

"Absolutely certain. There was no question of it. It was them, and I'm certain of what they're doing," Gwen replied.

They had just finished the milking, and now they were about to start making butter, churning the milk to separate it. Gwen was turning the handle, and Lisette was pouring in the milk from a large pail.

"But you'll only be certain if you can try it," Lisette said, and Gwen nodded.

"That's right, we need some of the milk. I'll know the taste immediately," she said.

"I'll go and buy some," Lisette said, and Gwen looked at her in surprise.

She had not expected Lisette to volunteer, but there was no reason why she should arouse any suspicion from Gwen's uncle or cousin. She was the perfect choice, and Gwen's heart skipped a beat at the thought of their exposing her uncle and his nefarious schemes.

"But… are you certain? I don't want to put you in any danger," she said, and Lisette shook her head.

"I can hold my own against any man. Besides, why would anyone be suspicious? I'm just a maid going to buy milk for her mistress, or a mother coming to buy milk for her baby. If they ask, I'll tell them I've just moved into rooms in a boarding house nearby and miss drinking fresh milk. I'll say I'm from the countryside originally, Berkshire, or somewhere like that. Besides, I'm sure your cousin wouldn't say no to a pretty face, would he?" she said, smiling at Gwen, who laughed, despite the danger Lisette was putting herself in.

But Lisette had always been a plucky creature, and when Madlen returned from the milk round with Harry, the two of them explained their plan.

"Madlen told me everything. I'm shocked, but I'm not surprised, either. It all makes sense, doesn't it – and we're the ones who pay the price for it, having the inspectors come knocking at the door. That and the poor people forced to drink it," Harry said, shaking his head sadly.

"And you're sure about doing this, Lisette?" Madlen asked.

"Really, I am. I don't want our dairy gaining a bad name because of those scoundrels. I'll go to Robinson's Dairy now, if you'll show me the way," she said, and Gwen nodded.

"We can show you. But we'll have to keep well hidden," she said, and Lisette nodded.

"I'll buy a small churn of milk, and I'll see what I can learn about what they're doing," she replied.

Despite Gwen's fears, it seemed Lisette was rather looking forward to her adventure, and with butter made, and their duties seen to at the dairy, the three of them set off through the snowy streets towards where Gwen and Madlen had followed their uncle and the others the previous evening.

"Owain has a small birthmark beneath his left eye. That's how you'll recognise him," Gwen said, as they got closer to Robinson's Dairy.

Lisette nodded, pulling her shawl up over her head as a headscarf.

"Alright, and I'll buy a small churn of milk," she said, as Gwen handed her some pennies.

"Be careful, Lisette. If they suspect anything they'll…" Gwen said, her words trailing off.

She knew what her uncle was capable of, and her

cousin. They were cruel men, and she did not doubt they were still the same as they had ever been.

"I'll be careful, and if I think they're suspicious… well, I'll just run for it," she said, and Gwen smiled.

"Thank you, Lisette," she said.

"I'm as angry as you are. They could kill someone. It doesn't bear thinking about," she said, and with that, she hurried off along the street towards the dairy.

Gwen and Madlen hid themselves in a builder's yard, peering out from behind a large pile of timber. They could see some distance along the street towards the dairy, watching as Lisette turned the corner and disappeared under the arch where the previous night the two of them had hidden in the shadows.

"She's very brave," Madlen said.

"She'll be alright. They can't possibly know her," Gwen replied.

"Unless they do know we're here. What if they've been watching the dairy all the time? If they were, they'd know Lisette by sight," Madlen said.

Gwen's heart skipped a beat, but it was too late for such fears now. Lisette would even now be talking to her uncle or cousin. It made her shudder to think of it. Six years had passed, but her memories remained vivid. She could picture her uncle and cousin, and Owain, too, even as she knew they would have aged. She wondered what life had been like for them since last they had been in one another's company. Where they had gone, what had they done?

"It won't come to that–they haven't been watching us. There's no reason for them to know we're even *in* London. As far as they're concerned, we stayed at the farm. Uncle Dawid probably thinks Reverend Llewelyn had us sent to the poorhouse or the orphanage," Gwen replied.

"Unless he knows Bryn's here. He does, doesn't he? He knows Bryn came to London," Madlen said, the panic rising in her voice.

"Oh, Madlen, don't say such things. It's too late now," Gwen replied, her heart beating fast as she realised they had been too quick to allow Lisette to enter the lion's den.

But Madlen was right. Her uncle and the others knew Bryn had come to the song school. They would know the Welsh chapel, and it would be a simple matter of asking around for any news of Gwen and her sister. They were often at the chapel and knew many of the congregation.

"We should go after her. We can't allow her to put herself in danger," Madlen said, and Gwen nodded.

They had been foolish–and too quick to act. Gwen knew Bryn would be angry with her, and she was about to leave the safety of the builder's yard, intent on causing a distraction to allow Lisette to escape. But as she emerged from behind the timber pile, she breathed a sigh of relief. Lisette was hurrying back along the street, carrying a small milk churn in her hand.

"What's wrong?" she asked, as Gwen hurried up to her.

"Oh… we realised… well, it doesn't matter now, I suppose. But… what happened?" Gwen asked, as they returned to their hiding place in the builder's yard.

"It was just as you described it – your uncle, your cousin, and your brother. They don't milk the cows there – they've got a herd out on the marshland near the Thames, and someone else looks after that side of things. Your cousin brings the milk to the dairy, and… well, obviously they didn't say any more than that. It's just the three of them. Your brother looked nervous, though," she said, and Gwen sighed.

"Poor Owain… I feel so guilty, but… the milk?" she said, glancing nervously at the small churn with its metal handle.

The top of the milk looked thick and creamy, but Gwen could only fear what it would be like when she tried it.

"I told them I was a maid to a woman who was very partial to boudoir biscuits. They said the milk was best for baking with because it's so creamy," Lisette said.

Gwen shuddered. She hardly dared to try it, but she knew she had to if she was to know for certain.

"Are you sure about this, Gwen?" Madlen asked, as Gwen raised the churn to her lips.

"I'll only taste a little–I'll know at once," she replied.

The thought of it made her feel sick–even the sight of it was enough for her to feel nauseous. She pictured Cadell and Owain gleefully adding handfuls of chalk to the milk churns at Talfryn Farm–just enough to turn it creamy. The thought made her shudder, and, taking a deep breath, she took a sip. Immediately, she spat it out. There was the distinctive taste, the cloying feeling in her mouth, the smell of the chalk. This was no longer milk; it was something else entirely…

"It's the same as it always was. Not everyone would notice it, but I know," Gwen said, and she poured the content of the churn onto the ground, where it ran down a nearby drain.

"Then we need to report it to the milk board–the inspectors can come at once," Lisette said.

"I shouldn't have poured it away, should I?" Gwen said, realising her mistake.

"It's alright. I told your cousin I'd come back. I

think he was quite taken by me," Lisette said, and Gwen smiled.

"Good, then we can bring the evidence with us. Let's go back and tell Harry. He can contact the inspectors and have them come here immediately," she said.

Cautiously, they left the builder's yard, hurrying back towards the song school. Gwen was eager to tell Bryn what they had discovered, even as she knew he might be angry at their placing Lisette in danger.

"You should've waited for me," he told them, after Lisette had recounted what had happened.

They had called at the song school, and Bryn had come at once from the dining room where the rest of the choir was having luncheon.

"Why? We didn't need a man with us. Besides, they know you. I'm the only one who could buy the milk," Lisette said, glaring at Bryn, who could not help but smile.

"I know, but… well, at least we know the truth now. You need to go there again and bring a sample of the milk back for the inspectors. It was foolish to have poured the first lot away, Gwen," Bryn said, and Gwen blushed, embarrassed at having been so foolish.

"I know… it just made me feel… ill," she said, and Bryn nodded.

"Well, it seems Lisette doesn't mind returning. Go back tomorrow and tell Harry to inform the inspectors. There's not a moment to lose. But you're certain they didn't suspect anything, Lisette?" he asked, and Lisette shook her head.

"Not at all. They said they don't normally sell such small quantities. Most of it gets distributed, but they didn't mind doing so for me," she said, raising her eyebrows.

Bryn smiled.

"No... I'm sure they didn't. I've got to go to a rehearsal now, but come back tomorrow and tell me what's happening," he said, and the three of them nodded.

Gwen felt foolish for her mistake with the milk, but she was determined to expose her uncle's continued wickedness. It had happened once, and now it was happening again. If her uncle and the others were not brought to justice, they would go on adulterating the milk, even if it killed someone.

"Don't worry about what Bryn said, Gwen. You poured the milk away out of disgust. I'll get some more tomorrow. They're expecting me," Lisette said as they left the song school, and Gwen nodded.

"I know, it's just... well, we should've waited for him, shouldn't we?" she said, but Lisette shook her head.

"What for? I don't need a man to follow me around and protect me," she said, and Gwen blushed.

"I didn't mean it like that," she said, and Lisette smiled.

"No, you meant Bryn himself, didn't you?" she replied.

"No… I mean, well… I suppose…" she stammered, and Madlen laughed.

"Oh, Gwen, why won't you admit it? You're in love with him, aren't you?" she said, and Gwen sighed.

She had not entirely admitted it to herself, but her sister was right. She *was* in love with Bryn, and despite trying her best to push such thoughts aside, they kept coming to the surface.

She wondered if she had always been in love with him. Childhood affection was giving way to deeper feelings, growing stronger by the day. The question of what lay ahead had brought to the fore those feelings she had tried to ignore, feelings she now knew would only grow stronger if she continued to ignore them.

"I… I suppose I am, but… you can't say anything, either of you," she exclaimed, and Lisette laughed.

"We won't say anything, Gwen. Why would we? But it's clear he's in love with you, too," Lisette replied, and Gwen looked at her in surprise.

"But… what do you mean?" she said, and Lisette rolled her eyes.

"Haven't you ever had a man fall in love with you?" she replied, and Gwen shook her head.

She did not know any other men, apart from Harry, and he had a sweetheart who lived in the Westend and worked in one of the theatres as a chorus girl. Her name was Hetty.

"No…" Gwen said, and Lisette smiled.

"No? Well, you have now. He never takes his eyes off you. He loves you, Gwen, and I think you feel the same way about him, too, don't you," she said, and Gwen smiled.

There was no point in denying it. She *did* feel the same way, though there was no telling if Bryn did, too.

"Well, I… I suppose I do, yes. But it's not been easy, and he's about to finish at the song school, too. I don't know what's going to happen next. And with all this business around the milk and my uncle," she said, shaking her head sadly.

"You'll find a way, I know you will," Lisette replied.

They returned to the dairy, finding Harry feeding the cows in the milking shed. The afternoon was drawing on and it would soon be dark.

Gwen was tired, not only from the exertions of the day, but from the shock of all that had happened

THE MILK MAID ORPHAN

since she had first seen her uncle from the steps of the chapel after the concert. So many memories had come to the fore–so many feelings long since pushed aside.

She had been thinking about her aunt, too, and wondering if things might have been different had she lived.

"I'll get in touch with the milk board, but they'll want proof if we're to accuse another dairy of adulterating their milk," Harry said.

"And we'll bring the proof tomorrow. I'm going back to Robinson's dairy to buy another churn," Lisette said, and Harry nodded.

"Alright, then, but be careful. I don't want any hint of our involvement getting out. Do you understand me?" he said, and Gwen and the others nodded.

"No one's going to find out it's us who reported them to the milk board, and even if they did, they'll all be in prison before long," Madlen said.

"And that's what you want, is it? Even for your brother to go to prison?" Harry said, glancing at Gwen, who sighed.

She did not want to see Owain punished in the same way as her uncle and Cadell. They had led him astray and caused him to become what he now was. Gwen blamed herself, even as she knew there was nothing more she could have done at the time.

Her brother had made his choice, but in Gwen's eyes, there was still a chance for him to redeem himself, if only he would take it.

"Owain could still have a change of heart," she said, and Harry nodded.

"Then you'll have to hope he has a good explanation for the milk board," he replied.

Gwen pondered these words, and her brother's plight, for the rest of the evening, her mind filled with thoughts of what might have been had Owain not sided with their uncle. As a young child, he had been no different to Madlen, but Cadell had been determined to have him for his own.

"Poor Owain," Gwen thought to herself. As she lay in bed that night, with the prospect of seeing her uncle finally brought to justice, she wondered if her brother, too, might find justice for himself against those who had wronged him, or would he maintain his misguided loyalty to the last?

OWAIN'S DILEMMA

"You didn't need to come with me, Gwen. I'll be quite alright," Lisette said, as she walked with Gwen and Madlen towards Robinson's Dairy.

"We couldn't let you go on your own," Gwen replied.

She still felt foolish for having poured away the adulterated milk from yesterday, and now she wanted to make sure the churn was returned to the dairy for milk inspectors to test.

"And what if you're seen?" Lisette replied.

"We hid in the builder's yard–no one saw us," Gwen said, and when they reached the archway, where the timber stacks lay in the yard beyond, they parted company.

Madlen had insisted on coming, too, and

despite the danger of what they were doing, Gwen was fascinated by the thought of seeing her uncle and the others again. She wanted to know what they had been doing since they had been in one another's company. She had so many questions, even as she doubted she would ever find the answers.

It was her brother who preoccupied her thoughts. She had every hope he might have changed, a sense of guilt coming over him, or even remorse for his crimes. If only she could speak to him…

"I won't be long, I promise," Lisette said, and now she walked on confidently down the street, leaving Gwen and Madlen to their hiding place.

"She's so brave," Madlen said.

"Well, they don't know her, do they? As far as they're concerned, she's just a customer come to buy milk, and you know how Cadell always was with attractive women," she said, shaking her head at the memory of her cousin's unwanted flirtations with any young woman who came to the farm.

It was about fifteen minutes later when Lisette returned. A nearby church clock had just struck the hour, and Gwen had been getting worried, fearing Lisette's identity might have been discovered. As she approached, Lisette had a grave look on her face.

"What happened?" Madlen asked.

"I got the milk," Lisette replied, holding up the churn.

"Let me try it," Gwen said, taking it from her before Lisette could reply.

Raising it to her lips, Gwen prepared herself for the cloying, sickly taste of the chalky milk, but as she took a sip, she was startled by the taste–fresh, creamy, delicious milk. It was pure, and there was no lingering taste of the chalk…

"But… I don't understand?" she said, and Lisette shook her head.

"Your uncle apologised to me. He told me I'd been given a bad batch that they only sold to restaurants and other commercial enterprises. He had been intending to pour away a batch, but got it mixed up with the one they intended to sell," she said, shaking her head.

Gwen sighed. She could hear her uncle saying such a thing, spinning a tale, making excuses. It was clear what had happened, the adulterated milk was intended to be sold only to those customers who were certain to use it in other products.

No right-thinking person could fail to recognise the adulterated milk in its pure form, and having made their apologies, Gwen's uncle and cousin could merely pretend the batch they had sold from was off.

"It's perfect–there's nothing wrong with it," Gwen said, shaking her head sadly.

"Then what are we going to do?" Madlen asked.

"I could go back again…" Lisette said, but Gwen shook her head.

She could only imagine her uncle had realised the possibility of a trick or had purposefully planned his scheme to only include those for whom there could be a guarantee of no repercussions. It would make it much harder for anyone, including the inspectors from the milk board, to catch them in the act of adulterating the milk.

"No, you can't go back. That would be foolish," she said.

"But what are we going to do?" Madlen said, and Gwen took a deep breath.

"We're going to talk to Owain," she replied. Her mind was made up, even as she knew the risk she was about to take.

* * *

"It's a bad idea, Gwen. You know what he's like," Bryn said, shaking his head.

"But it's the only way, Owain. I've got to try. I can't let them get away with it," Gwen replied.

They were sitting in Bryn's sitting room at the song school. As one of the senior boys, he had his own set looking out over Saint James' Place–a pleasantly furnished sitting room, where he could receive guests, with a small bedroom leading off it. Gwen had come to tell him what had happened, and he had listened patiently, shaking his head with a sigh when she had concluded.

"But Gwen… it's not your fight. You tried, and I'm proud of you for that, but… well, if there's no proof, there's no proof, is there?" he said.

"But if only I can find the proof… Bryn, don't you remember how guilty I felt?" she said, and Bryn raised his eyebrows.

"And didn't I always tell you not to feel guilty?" he replied.

"I know, but… I can't help it. The thought of someone dying… the thought of someone having already died. It fills me with dread, Bryn. I was powerless to do anything about it before, and I still feel guilty for it, whatever you say. But this… I can do something about it, and if Owain can be persuaded…" she said, but Bryn interrupted her.

"Or if Owain hasn't changed at all and goes running to your uncle and cousin… what then? Do you think they'll sit idly by and let you ruin their little scheme? I think not, Gwen. They'll be after you–after all of us," Bryn said.

Gwen sighed. She knew he was right. But was Owain still siding with her uncle and cousin? She thought back to the tone of his voice, and to what Lisette had said, too.

Perhaps there was something–a difference come over him, a question in his mind, a change of heart. He was her brother, and Gwen had always had a sense of maternal closeness to him, especially after the death of their aunt.

Madlen had washed her hands entirely of him, telling Gwen she was foolish if she thought Owain would ever change. But in her heart, Gwen knew she had to try. She had to do it, if only to put her mind at rest.

"I'm not asking you to come with me, Bryn," Gwen said, and Bryn sighed.

"I don't like the thought of you going alone," he said.

"I'll be alright. I'll wait somewhere until he's alone. I won't let my uncle or cousin see me; I promise. But I've got to try. I promise I'll be careful," she said, and Bryn nodded.

"You were always the same, Gwen. When you got an idea into your head, you couldn't be dissuaded from it–like singing in the choir. It's something I've always admired about you. But... well, now I'm not so sure," he replied.

"You're right–I won't be dissuaded. But please, won't you give me your blessing?" she said, and Bryn smiled.

"Since you're going to do it anyway, I suppose so," he replied, and Gwen grinned at him.

"Thank you," she said.

For a moment, they stood looking at one another, their gaze fixed, and Gwen felt the blush rising in her cheeks. She remembered what Lisette had said, and Madlen, and she wondered what he was feeling, what he was thinking…

"Gwen… I know we haven't talked about… what happens next, after I leave here, I mean," Bryn said, and Gwen was surprised as he reached out and took her hand in his.

"I… I wasn't sure what would happen," she said, even as she knew she had given it a great deal of thought.

It had saddened her to think there could be a parting of ways between them–a separation forced by circumstance, rather than desire. But now her feelings for him made it impossible to comprehend anything but the two of them being together. She did not want to see him go, and tears now welled up in her eyes.

"Me, neither. But I know… wherever I go, I want it to be with you," he said.

Gwen's heart skipped a beat. She could hardly believe what he was saying, even as these were the words she had longed to hear.

"Do you mean it?" she asked, and he nodded.

"I've thought a lot about it and about you, too. I suppose I was upset today because… well, because I care so deeply about you, and the thought of you entering the lion's den, so to speak, was just too awful to comprehend," he replied.

A tear rolled down Gwen's cheek at his words, and she nodded.

"I know, and I'm sorry. You know I can be headstrong," she said, and he laughed.

"Oh, I know that. But when this is all over, when we've proved what your uncle and cousin have been doing… well, perhaps we can talk about the future, too?" he said, and Gwen smiled.

"I'd like that," she replied, and leaning forward, he kissed her lightly on the cheek.

A shiver ran through her, her feelings towards him no longer confused. If this was not love, then Gwen knew she would never know love. He meant everything to her, and if it was not for Bryn, her life would be far from happy.

"I'll be waiting for you, but please, be back before nightfall," he said, and Gwen nodded.

"I will, I promise," she said, and with a last smile and a blush, they said their farewells.

Outside, snow was falling heavily, and smog was drifting through the streets. A distant church clock was striking noon, and Gwen hurried towards Robinson's Dairy.

She did not have a definite plan, though she knew she had to try to speak with Owain alone. If her uncle or cousin saw her, they would only grow angry, and Gwen knew she would be in danger.

Owain was different, or so she wanted to believe. His behaviour–the terrible things he had said and done–was the result of Cadell's influence. Things could have been very different. They should have been very different.

"And perhaps they still could be," she thought to herself, as she came in the sight of the street leading to Robinson's Dairy, pausing at the arch into the builder's yard. She did not want to get too close lest she be seen by her uncle or cousin, but nor could she remain too far away for fear of not seeing Owain at all.

Gwen knew nothing of their routine, or even if Owain would be at the dairy at that time. Some men were moving timber in the builder's yard, and one of them eyed her suspiciously as she approached.

"No urchins. Be gone with you. No beggars," he said, but Gwen shook her head.

"I'm no urchin, and I'm certainly not a beggar. I'm a milk maid," she said, and the man laughed.

"Are you looking for the dairy? It's down the street there, Robinson's Dairy. But I doubt they'll take kindly to your appearing there. Mr. Parry doesn't like visitors," the man said, shaking his head.

"I'm looking for someone, Owain, his nephew," Gwen replied, and the man nodded.

"Ah, yes... Owain... you might find him the tavern on Longbarton Street, near the canal. Though I'd be careful if I was you, a young pretty girl unaccompanied," he said, glancing at the others, who laughed.

"Thank you," Gwen replied, and the builder pointed her in the direction of the tavern, repeating his warning, even as he and the others continued to laugh.

Gwen set off towards the tavern, taking a circuitous route and getting lost several times as she navigated the back streets around the dairy–a maze of tenements, warehouses, and courtyards, their grim facades gazing forlornly down at her.

The tavern was called *The Fighting Cocks*, its creaking sign depicting two roosters facing one another with stern expressions on their faces. The door was approached by a flight of stone steps, and the tavern itself was built next to the canal, hemmed in by warehouses on either side.

The windows were grimy, but from inside, the sound of an accordion could be heard, and the bawdy voice of a woman singing...

> *"Here's a health to the Queen and a lasting peace*
> *To faction an end, to wealth increase.*
> *Come, let us drink it while we have breath,*

For there's no drinking after death.
And he that will this health deny,
Down among the dead men, down among the dead men,
Down, down, down, down;
Down among the dead men, let him lie!"

THE SONG WENT on for several more verses, and gradually the occupants of the tavern joined in, until the echo of the song filled the air. Gwen shuddered, wondering what sort of place she had come to.

As if in answer to her question, the door of the tavern now opened and several men stumbled out, their arms around one another, swaying from side to side.

"Here's a health to the Queen," one of the called out, and the other dropped the bottle he was carrying, the glass shattering on the steps.

The men cursed one another, swaying up the steps, as Gwen stepped back fearfully.

"A pretty girl, a pretty girl, indeed," one of the said, leering towards Gwen, who shrank back against the wall of the warehouse next to the inn.

"Leave her be. She'll be taken, won't she?" the third one said, and they stumbled off together, repeating the words of the song.

Gwen's heart was beating fast, but she was

determined to find her brother, and cautiously, she made her way down the steps towards the door of the inn. The singer, if she could be described as such, had once again launched into a rendition of another drinking song, and Gwen stepped into the taproom, not attracting any attention to herself at first, as she looked around her in search of Owain.

"There's no touting for trade in here, miss," a man behind the counter said, pointing to the door.

Gwen's eyes grew wide with horror at the thought of what he was suggesting, and she shook her head, approaching the counter.

"You misunderstand me. I'm looking for my brother, Owain Parry," she said.

The man, whom Gwen could only assume to be the landlord, smiled, nodding towards the dark recesses of the inn, beyond where the singer was standing on an upturned barrel whilst a man sitting on a stool played the accordion.

"I didn't know he had a sister, and not a pretty one like you. He's back there," he said, and Gwen nodded.

"Thank you," she replied, taking a deep breath.

The landlord had given no indication of whether her brother was with her uncle or cousin, and now she made her way cautiously into the shadows, where a haze of tobacco smoke filled the air, and several groups of men sat huddled around tables drinking and whispering to one another.

Gwen's heart was beating fast, and Bryn's words echoed in her mind–he could be just the same as he always was…

"But I've got to try. Not just for him, but for all those poor people poisoned by the milk," she told herself, as now she saw a figure hunched over a tankard, sitting sideways on at table right at the back of the tavern against the wall.

Gwen's heart skipped a beat. It was Owain. By her reckoning, he was not sixteen years old, and from the way he was sitting, he looked tall and lanky. His hair was unkempt and there was the hint of a beard on his chin and cheeks.

Gwen had only seen him at a distance on the day she had followed him and her uncle and cousin to the dairy, but now she was able to study him better for a few moments, keeping to the shadows as she did so. He was drinking alone, and there was no sign of either her uncle or cousin.

"Owain?" Gwen said, and her brother looked up, startled to hear his name.

He stared at Gwen through the gloom, his eyes wide with astonishment.

"Gwen?" he exclaimed, and she nodded.

"It's me," she replied, approaching him as he rose to his feet.

He towered over her, but Gwen was not afraid of him. He was her brother, and despite his many faults, she still loved him. She had never stopped loving him, despite the things he had said and done to her. But the look on his face was not the cruel, callous look she had seen in Cadell's eyes so often, but the sorrowful look of one harbouring regrets. One who carried a burden.

"But... what are you doing here? Where... what became of you?" he said.

"There's a lot for us to talk about–if you'll do so," Gwen said, for she was still wary of him, even as he now beckoned for her to sit.

"I don't understand why you're here. Did you come from the valley?" he asked, and Gwen shook her head.

She had nothing to hide, and now she explained something of what had happened to her and Madlen since the last the three of them had been in one another's company. Owain listened, shaking his head in astonishment as Gwen's story came to an end.

"We thought you'd stayed... Uncle Dawid assumed Reverend Llewelyn would send you to the poorhouse or the orphanage. We never thought... and you've been in London the whole time?" Owain asked, and Gwen nodded.

"That's right, yes working at the dairy with

THE MILK MAID ORPHAN

Madlen. But what about you? What happened after you left the farm that night?" she asked.

Her brother shook his head and sighed.

"What happened was… well… I wish I'd never gone. I was foolish, Gwen," he said, and Gwen reached out and took his hand in hers.

"You *were* foolish, yes, but you were young, too. It was Cadell, and Uncle Dawid, they led you into it," Gwen replied.

There was a sincerity in her brother's voice–a regret, and a sense of fear, too.

"And now… oh, I'm in over my head, Gwen. The things we must do. It's terrible," he said, shaking his head.

"But where did you go when you left the farm? Did you come to London?" Gwen asked, for he had still not explained what had happened since they had parted company.

"We went north to Manchester. Uncle Dawid took a job in an abattoir. We used different names, but now… his plan was always to get back into the milk business. He sells to the large businesses–hotels and restaurants. He knew they'd use the milk to make other things with. Then there's no telling the quality of it. We mix the chalk in like before. We've been here just over a year. Cadell and I worked at the abattoir, too. We lived in a hovel, a tenement, in just one room. I miss the farm," Owain said, shaking his head.

It was perhaps the first time he had been able to voice his feelings, and Gwen could only feel sorry for him. Sorry for what her uncle and cousin had done to him. He had been too young to understand, and too easily led astray. The same could be said now, and it seemed her uncle and cousin still had a hold over him.

"You've got to testify against them, Owain, you've got to get out," Gwen said, and her brother stared at her in horror.

"You don't know what you're saying, Gwen. I can't," he said, and Gwen reached out and took his hand in hers.

"I've never given up on the hope of you finding the right path again, Owain. I want you back. I want my brother back," she said, and Owain sighed.

"Gwen… I'm sorry for the things I did — for what I said to you. They were cruel. You tried to look after me, you tried to warn me, but I wouldn't listen," he said, and Gwen smiled weakly.

"Cadell was the one you listened to. I understand, Owain, but it doesn't have to be like that anymore, does it?" Gwen replied.

Owain shook his head.

"I don't know… I don't know what I can do… I'm

trapped here, Gwen," he said, a note of desperation in his voice.

Gwen squeezed his hand. She could only feel sorry for him, despite the things he had said and done. There was no doubting his regret–the half empty tankard, a sign of his sorrows, drowned at the back of a dingy tavern.

"It doesn't have to be like this, Owain. You can have a better life than this, if you want it, that is," Gwen replied.

But her brother shook his head.

"They'd say I was as much a part of it as they are," Owain replied.

"But not back then you weren't. You couldn't have been. And if you testify against them… perhaps you'll be looked on kindly. It's Uncle Dawid who's responsible, and Cadell, too," Gwen said, and Owain sighed.

"I need to get back. They'll be wondering where I am. I'm glad I saw you, Gwen. You look very well. Tell Madlen… tell her I'm sorry," he said, rising to his feet.

Gwen caught his hand, imploring him to stay.

"Please, Owain. Won't you think about it? It doesn't have to be like this. You know it doesn't," Gwen said, but her brother shook his head.

"You'll find me in here most days, in the afternoon.

We can talk again, Gwen, but… I don't think there's much more to say, do you? I can't turn back the clock. If I could, perhaps I wouldn't be in this dreadful mess. I'm sorry," he said, and with that, he was gone.

Gwen sighed, watching as he hurried out of the inn. The singer was in the midst of a rousing chorus, and Gwen left unnoticed, wondering what to do next.

Having seen the fear in her brother's eyes and heard the regret in his voice, Gwen knew she could not stand idly by and allow him to be dragged down alongside her uncle and cousin. The net was closing, and Gwen was determined to do all she could to help her brother, even as she knew the danger lying ahead…

THE CHRISTMAS CELEBRATION

"*And* do you think you can convince him?" Bryn asked after Gwen had recounted what had happened at the tavern that afternoon.

"I don't know... I hope so. But he's terrified of them, Bryn. He thinks he'll be held responsible, too– and punished," Gwen replied, sighing, and shaking her head.

They were sitting in Bryn's rooms at the song school. It was snowing outside, and Gwen was glad of the warmth of the fire after her walk back through the cold. Bryn had been practising the music the choir would be singing on Christmas Day in the chapel, but he had set it aside to listen to Gwen's story. Now he sat opposite her by the fire, pondering what she had just told him.

"But he will be punished–he's had a hand in it,

and the judge won't care much for the nuances," Bryn replied.

"I know, but... perhaps if he was to testify against them, there might be some leniency," Gwen said.

She knew she was being wishful in her thinking. Owain was culpable. He had adulterated the milk with their uncle and cousin, and the three of them were in it together.

In meeting her brother for the first time in so many years, Gwen had glimpsed a vision of what he might have been like, had circumstances been different. She wanted to believe he could change and that he could be a different person to the one who had behaved so cruelly in years gone by.

"I wouldn't count on it. But at least... well, can you trust him not to tell your uncle or cousin he met you?" Bryn asked.

Gwen nodded. Her brother had told her he would be back at the tavern the following afternoon, and despite knowing what her uncle and cousin were capable of, Gwen felt certain Owain would not tell them he had met her.

"I think so, besides... I don't know what to do next. He said he wouldn't testify, but... do we still report it?" Gwen asked.

She knew her uncle was clever. The trick with the pure milk, and selling only to those businesses who would use the milk to make other things, rather than to drink. Proving the case would not be easy, not without the testament of Owain to support their claims.

"I don't see how we can. There's no proof, is there?" Bryn replied.

Gwen shook her head. She was angry to think her uncle and cousin would get away with what they were doing. As a child, Gwen had been powerless to stop them, and now she felt powerless once again.

"None at all, no. I just... well, I wish there was something more we could do," she replied.

Bryn rose to his feet, crossing the hearth and looking down at her with a reassuring smile.

"And we can, but we must bide our time. It's nearly Christmas. We've got the song school party to look forward to, and the services on Christmas Day. You will come, won't you? To the Christmas party, I mean," he said, and Gwen nodded.

She and Madlen had been invited to the song school Christmas party by the choirmaster. He knew she and Bryn were on friendly terms, and the two sisters had bought new ribbons for their hair and embroidered a pattern of holly and ivy onto two old shawls they had found in a dressmaker's shop a few weeks previously.

"I've been looking forward to it for weeks. I'm sorry, Bryn. I know I shouldn't be worried about these things, but I can't help it. It makes me so angry to think of my uncle and cousin… and what they've done to Owain, too," Gwen said, and Bryn reached out and took Gwen by the hand.

"It'll be alright, I promise," he said, and she looked up at him and smiled.

"You say so with such confidence. But I believe you," she said, and he smiled back at her.

"It will be, Gwen. Now… I need to practice my solo. Will you stay and listen?" he asked, and Gwen nodded, for she could think of nothing she would like better than to do so…

* * *

"I wish I was invited to a Christmas party," Lisette said, watching as Gwen and Madlen readied themselves for the evening's festivities at the song school.

They had put the ribbons in their hair and had finished embroidering their shawls with holly and ivy. It was exciting, and Gwen was looking forward to dancing with Bryn, and to the promised feast awaiting them.

"Perhaps next year. You should get to know the choir better. They're all delightful," Gwen said, and Lisette smiled.

"I'm Catholic. They won't take kindly to me stepping into their chapel," she said, shaking her head and laughing.

THE MILK MAID ORPHAN

"Do I look alright, Gwen?" Madlen asked, and Gwen pretended to inspect her sister like a regimental sergeant major.

"Shoulders up, stand straight," she said, and Madlen giggled.

"Well, do I?" she asked, and Gwen nodded.

"You look lovely, Madlen," she replied.

"And so do you, Gwen," her sister said.

The party was to take place in the song school dining room, and Gwen and Madlen now set off from the dairy, hurrying through the snowy street, and finding the windows of the song school lit up with candles and lanterns. A large wreath of greenery adorned the door, and through the dining-room windows, Gwen could see the choir boys already enjoying the celebrations.

"You look very pretty," Bryn said, as he welcomed them a few moments later.

"Thank you," Gwen replied, blushing, as he ushered her and Madlen inside.

The dining room was decorated with paper chains and greenery, and a large tree created a spectacular centrepiece, its branches hung with all manner of decorations, and adorned with candles. A trestle table, covered in a white cloth, stood to one side, laden with all manner of good things to eat, including an enormous trifle in a glass dish at its centre.

There were sandwiches, jam tarts, and all manner of other cakes and confections, sweet and savoury, along with jugs of cordial and milk. Some of the choirboys also played musical instruments. The choirmaster was directing them in the playing of Christmas carols, harmonized by the other boys, all of whom were dressed in their Sunday clothes, along with paper crowns in all manner of different colours.

"Isn't it wonderful?" Madlen exclaimed, looking around her in delight.

"It's going to be great fun. I'm so glad you could come," Bryn said, slipping his arm into Gwen's.

"I'm glad we could come, too," she replied, as he led them across the room to chairs by the hearth, where a large log was burning brightly.

"It's a yule log. We used to have a yule log at the farm. Do you remember, Madlen?" Gwen said, and Madlen nodded.

"We used to have such lovely Christmases, before Aunt Cerian died," Madlen replied.

Gwen smiled. She had been thinking about her aunt a great deal lately. Aunt Cerian would not have given up on Owain. She saw the good in everyone, though she would have been horrified at the thought of what had become of her own husband and son.

Had Gwen's aunt lived, Gwen knew the milk would never have been adulterated. She had been a good woman, possessed of strong Christian values, and her faith had been at the centre of all she did.

"We did, yes, and it's nice to remember her, isn't it?" Gwen replied.

"I was thinking about my grandmother the other day. She'd never have believed it–me, at the song school in London. She lived her whole life in the valley. It was all she knew. She'd never have imagined a world like this," he said.

"But she'd have been so proud of you, Bryn. I can just picture the smile on her face. She was a wonderful woman. I miss her, too," Gwen said, thinking fondly of Bryn's grandmother.

The choirmaster called the room to order, standing on a chair, and dressed in a most peculiar, patterned smoking jacket with a paper crown on his head.

"Good afternoon, everyone, and what a jolly time we're having. If only it could be Christmas every day. You've all worked exceedingly hard this year, and particularly in the run up to Christmas, and this is my way of thanking you for your hard work and dedication to the choir and the music. I hope you all have a very jolly time. We'll tuck into the tea now, shall we?" he said, clapping his hands together as the choirboys now eagerly hurried forward to the tea table.

Gwen smiled. The choirmaster, Mr. Jones, was

always so strict with the boys, and yet it seemed the Christmas spirit had quite overcome him, as now he joined the others in piling his plate high with the treats and fancies from the tea table.

"Come along, we'd better tuck in, too. There'll be nothing left, otherwise," Bryn said, and Gwen and Madlen followed him across the room to the tea table.

The trifle was proving particularly popular amongst the younger boys, and Gwen took a plate, helping herself to fish paste sandwiches and jam tarts. Madlen did the same, and they returned to the hearth whilst Bryn talked to some of the older boys and Mr. Jones ushered the younger ones to sit by the tree, where presents were laid out–one for each of them.

"Owain always enjoyed Christmas at the farm with Aunt Cerian," Gwen said.

Madlen rolled her eyes.

"Oh, Gwen, he's never going to be like that again," she said, shaking her head.

Gwen had recounted the story of her encounter with Owain to her sister, but Madlen had refused to believe he had changed.

"But he could be, Madlen. It's not an impossibility. I saw him, you didn't. He's not the same as he used to be. He regrets what happened. I know he does," Gwen said, but Madlen only shook her head.

"I don't want to talk about him, Gwen. He'll never testify against Uncle Dawid or Cadell. Even if he did, he'd still be held responsible, at least in one way or another," Madlen replied.

"But we've got to try, Madlen. He's a lost soul. Isn't it right we do something to help him?" Gwen said, but Madlen shook her head.

"You can do something to help him, Gwen. I'd rather never see him again. And you know what Bryn thinks, too," Madlen replied.

Gwen *did* know what Bryn thought, and she knew he did not want her getting mixed up with her brother–nor her uncle and cousin. But even if she had wanted to, Gwen could not rid herself of a desire to do something to help her brother, and she had every intention of returning to *The Fighting Cocks* and searching him out.

"I know, and I don't want to upset him, but... I just want to do what's best for Owain, too," Gwen replied.

"We can't help him, Gwen. He made his bed, let him lie in it," Madlen replied.

Gwen was about to continue arguing when a sudden commotion caused her to look up. Several of the younger members of the choir were clutching at their stomachs, lying back on the rug by the Christmas tree, and moaning loudly.

"What's happened, boys? What's wrong?" the

choirmaster exclaimed, hurrying over to them with a concerned expression on his face.

Others, too, were now complaining, and around the room a dozen or so of the children were clutching at their stomachs, their faces pale, their expressions dazed. Bryn hurried over to Gwen and Madlen with a worried expression on his face.

"It's something they've eaten–all of them," he said, and Gwen glanced at the tea table, gripped by a sudden fear.

"The trifle?" she said, glancing around the room at the sick children, all of whom had a half-eaten bowl of trifle at their side.

"But… what could be wrong with it?" Bryn said, and Gwen raised her eyebrows.

"The milk–the cream, the custard… it's all milk," she said, and Bryn's eyes grew wide with fear.

"We need to find out where it came from," he said, and leaving Madlen and Mr. Jones to tend to the sick choirboys, Gwen and Bryn hurried down to the kitchens.

Mrs. Brooks, the cook, was sitting with her feet up by the fire, and she looked up in surprise as Gwen and Bryn burst in.

"Whatever's the matter? They can't have finished yet. I've only just sat down. I'll send one of the scullery maids up to clear things away," she said.

"It's not that, Mrs. Brooks. They're ill, all the boys

THE MILK MAID ORPHAN

are ill, the ones who ate the trifle," Bryn said, and the cook stared at him in astonishment.

"The trifle? What are you talking about? They can't be ill. I've been making the same trifle for years–always the same, my own madeira cake, homemade jam, freshly made custard, whipped cream. I won't hear of it. What's happened to them?" she said, fixing Bryn with an angry glare.

"They've got stomach cramps; they're writhing around on the floor. They're all ill, Mrs. Brooks," Bryn said, and the cooking threw her hands up in horror.

"Oh, Lord have mercy. I've never poisoned anyone," she exclaimed, tears welling up in her eyes.

The commotion had attracted the other servants, and news of the goings on in the dining room now spread.

"No one's accusing you of poisoning anyone, Mrs. Brooks, but where did you get the milk from to make the custard? And the cream to whip for the top?" Gwen asked.

She already knew the answer. It was Harry Bartlett who supplied the song school with milk and dairy products. Gwen had made the butter spread on the bread for the sandwiches, but even as she thought the answer obvious, Mrs. Brooks' eyes grew wide and fearful.

"That's it. The milk and cream. Harry Bartlett

didn't have enough. He told me he'd send you or your sister over, but then he couldn't find you, and… oh, I was getting impatient. I bought it from a wholesaler–Robinson's Dairy," she said, glancing towards the cold store, where two large churns stood on the flagstone floor.

Gwen hurried over, glancing into the first churn and sniffing. She could smell the chalk, even as the milk appeared fresh and creamy. Glancing back towards Bryn, Gwen nodded.

"Chalk," she said, and the cook gave a cry.

"Chalk? In the milk, you mean?" she exclaimed, and Gwen nodded.

"They add it to make it creamy, but too much and it's poisonous–it could be deadly," she said, and Mrs. Brooks promptly fainted.

One of the scullery maids rushed to fetch some water, and Gwen and Bryn helped the cook into her chair. As she opened her eyes, she gazed up at them with a sorrowful expression on her face.

"It's too terrible for words," she said, and Gwen took her hand in hers and squeezed it.

"But it's not your fault, Mrs. Brooks. You weren't to know. They sold you the milk on a lie – they're the ones responsible, not you," Gwen said, patting Mrs. Brooks' hand.

"I'll go up and see what's happening," Bryn said, and Gwen nodded.

THE MILK MAID ORPHAN

"I'll stay with her," she said, pulling up a stool to sit at Mrs. Brooks' chairside.

Bryn was gone for around half an hour, and when he returned, he reported a total of fourteen choirboys having fallen ill from eating the trifle.

"Mr. Jones and the matrons are putting them to bed, but they're all very ill. There's no doubting the source – all of them ate the trifle. We were lucky," he said, shaking his head.

Mrs. Brooks let out another wail. She had been alternating between wailing and sobbing, and Gwen had done her best to comfort her, telling her it was not her fault, and no one would blame her for what had happened.

"Those poor children. Twenty years I've worked here twenty years and not once have I caused any of them any harm with my cooking. What will people say?" she said, shaking her head and dabbing at her eyes with the handkerchief Gwen had given her.

"They won't say anything, Mrs. Brooks. You've done nothing wrong; I assure you," Bryn said, but the cook was inconsolable.

Eventually, they left her in the hands of the scullery maids and returned upstairs. Madlen was waiting for them in the hallway, and it seemed the happy Christmas atmosphere was forgotten.

The trifle stood ominously on the table in the dining room, and Gwen approached it, leaning forward to sniff. The smell of chalk was distinctive, mixed with the more pleasant scent of vanilla and dried fruit.

"It's the trifle–there's no doubt about it," she said, shaking her head.

"And the milk came from Robinson's Dairy," Bryn replied.

"Well, that's all we need to know, isn't it? The milk board can close them down, and when they discover who's running it…" she said, but Gwen shook her head.

"Uncle Dawid would just deny everything. He'd say it was a bad batch. He'd probably blame the cows themselves," Gwen replied.

"But if your cousin's conscience could be pricked? Bring him here and show him what the adulterated milk did to the children. One of them could've died, Bryn said, and Gwen nodded.

"You're right. If this doesn't make him change his mind, nothing will," she replied.

"But I'm coming with you this time," Bryn said.

"And so am I," Madlen added.

Gwen smiled at them, grateful for their offer, even as she doubted the matter would change her brother's mind. Owain had made his decision, but if there was still a trace of the decency instilled in him by their aunt, she wondered if perhaps he might still have a change of heart.

"He'll have been in *The Fighting Cocks* this afternoon. It's only just six O'clock. If we hurry, perhaps we can catch him," Gwen said, and the other nodded.

Wrapping up against the cold, and with the Christmas party having ended abruptly, they headed out into the chilly evening air, heading in the direction of the tavern. Gwen's heart was beating fast, and she was fearful they could so easily return to tragedy, the thought of it sending a shiver down her spine.

"If one of them dies… oh, it's just too awful to contemplate," Bryn said, as they hurried through the snowy streets.

"Whatever happens, my uncle's responsible for poisoning them," Gwen replied, and with a fresh sense of determination, she urged them on, hoping Owain's conscience could be pricked, and justice could be done.

A BROTHERLY REUNION

"You two stay here, I'll go in," Bryn said, as they arrived at the top of the steps leading down to *The Fighting Cocks*.

Gwen raised her eyebrows.

"I've already been in there, Bryn. If anyone's likely to be noticed, it's a well-dressed young man from a song school, and not a milkmaid," she replied, and Bryn blushed.

"I just… I want to do something, Gwen," he replied, and Gwen smiled.

"You've already done more than enough. We'll all go in. I want Madlen to make peace with her brother," Gwen said, turning to Madlen, who scowled.

"It's him who should make peace with us, Gwen, not the other way around," she said, but Gwen shook her head.

"No, Madlen, he's our brother. We can't forget that," she said, and Madlen sighed.

"You always were the one with better morals," she said, and Gwen laughed.

"It's all that singing in the choir. Reverend Llewelyn's sermons obviously had an impact on me," she replied.

They made their way down the slippery steps to the door of the tavern. There was no sound of singing coming from inside, and Gwen opened the door cautiously. The scene was much the same as before, men sitting huddled over tankards at tables, whispering to one another. One group was playing cards, another sharing a joke, smiling at one another as they exchanged a joke. The landlord was standing behind the counter, cleaning glasses, and he looked up at Gwen as she and the others entered, jerking his head towards the dark recesses of the tavern.

"He's here," he said, and Gwen nodded.

"Thank you," she replied, slipping her hand into Madlen's.

They made their way past the other tables, all eyes in the tavern following them. Owain was sitting in the same place as before, hunched over a tankard, and as they approached, he looked up in surprise.

"Gwen? Madlen? Bryn?" he exclaimed, rising to his feet.

"I suppose you haven't heard what's happened?"

Gwen asked, and her brother looked at her in surprise.

"I don't know what you mean," he said, and Madlen glared at him.

"The children at the song school. All of them poisoned by the milk in the trifle. The milk you sold them," she exclaimed, banging her fist down angrily on the table.

Gwen raised her hand, as Owain's eyes grew wide with fear.

"The song school? But… I didn't know… we don't normally…" he stammered.

"You're lucky none of the children died, not yet, at least," Bryn said, shaking his head.

There was a genuine look of fear in Owain's eyes, and he shook his head before running his hands through his hair as though in despair.

"It wasn't meant to be like that. I didn't want to poison anyone. But they kept adding the chalk. I told them it was too much. Those poor children," he said, looking up at Gwen with tears in his eyes.

"Owain, please. You've got to testify against Uncle Dawid and Cadell. If you don't, think what could happen next," Gwen said.

Owain looked terrified, and Madlen folded her arms and gave an exasperated sigh.

"You see… he won't do it. He's a coward," she said, but Gwen shook her head.

"No, he's not. He's had a lifetime of being under the control of Cadell and our uncle. Now's your chance to put things right," she said, staring at Owain imploringly.

He looked from one to the other, and tears now rolled down his cheeks.

"I never meant to hurt anyone; I swear it. It wasn't meant to be like this. None of it was. When we started doing it again, we said we'd be careful," he said.

"Careful not to get caught," Madlen said, rolling her eyes.

But Gwen reached out and took her brother's hand in hers. She wanted him to know she believed him and wanted to help him.

"Please, Owain. You've got to do the right thing. We've got the evidence we need. If you tell the milk board what happened, the consequences for you won't be anything like they will be for Uncle Dawid and Cadell. They're the ones who deserve to be punished, Owain, not you," Gwen said.

She wanted him to believe her. She wanted him to do the right thing even as she could see, he was torn between his head and his heart. He would be punished, there was no doubt of that, but better that than to find himself later charged with murder…

"I know… and I'm sorry," Owain said.

"You see—he's a coward. He won't do anything," Madlen said, shaking her head.

"Give him a chance," Bryn replied, and Gwen now squeezed her brother's hand, imploring him to do the right thing.

She could picture him as a child sitting on their aunt's knee, smiling as she sang a lullaby to him. There was good in him, there was no doubting that, and Gwen wanted only to save him from a fate far worse than this one…

"You've made some mistakes, Owain, but it's not too late to change, not now," Gwen said, and Owain nodded.

"I… I'll do it," he said, letting out a deep sigh as he spoke.

Gwen smiled at him.

"Thank you," she said, and stepping forward, she put her arms around him.

He did the same, and for a moment, they stood in silence, embracing one another. As Gwen stepped back, she glanced at Madlen, who still had a sceptical look on her face.

"Do you really mean it, Owain?" Madlen asked, and their brother nodded.

"I promise you, yes," he said, and Madlen sighed.

"You said some terrible things, Owain. You hurt us both. But… if Gwen can forgive you, so can I," she said, and stepping forward, she held out her arms to him, embracing him, as Gwen glanced at Bryn and smiled.

"You're doing the right thing, Owain," Bryn said, and he held out his hand to Gwen's brother, who took it and smiled nervously.

"I still don't know how I can of any real use," he said, but Gwen shook her head.

"It's your word, Bryn. Once the milk board hears your testimony, they can't possibly do anything else but have Uncle Dawid and Cadell arrested. We've got the evidence from the trifle. Mrs. Brooks, the cook at the song school, still has half a churn of adulterated milk. We told her to keep it as evidence. No… this time, there's no getting away for them," Gwen replied.

"And what about me?" Owain asked.

Gwen did not know, but she felt certain there would be leniency, given what her brother would be able to tell the inspectors he knew. He had only been a child when their uncle had taken him and had known nothing other than the cruel words and actions of the two embittered men.

"We'll do whatever we can to help you, Owain, I promise," Bryn said, and Owain nodded.

"It's good of you to say so, but I doubt… well, you're right, Gwen. I couldn't live with myself if I knew I was responsible for someone dying, and if it was a child... no, it can't go on. It's not right. It was never right. I suppose I always pretended it wasn't really happening. It was just a little chalk–that's what Cadell always said. It does no harm to anyone... but it's not true. I know better now," Owain replied, and Gwen nodded.

She took his hand in hers, glad to have her brother back–glad to think he was doing the right thing. There was still a great task ahead of them, but with Owain's testimony, and the evidence of the trifle and the milk churn, no one could doubt what her uncle and cousin had been involved in.

"Come back to the dairy with us. Don't go back to Uncle Dawid and Cadell," Gwen said.

Owain looked uncertain for a moment, but Madlen now seized him by the hand.

"Oh, for goodness's sake, Owain. You look like you haven't had a proper meal in weeks, and you need a haircut, too, and a wash. Come along, I won't have my brother go without," she said, and Owain smiled.

"I really am sorry," he said, but Gwen shook her head.

"I think we're all sorry, Owain. But there's a chance to put it right now, isn't there?" Gwen said, and Owain nodded.

It felt as though a great burden had been lifted

from her, from all of them. She had her brother back, and for all his faults, and all that had passed between them, she was glad of it.

"They'll look for me–they'll suspect something," he said, but Gwen shook her head.

"You wait until you meet Lisette. She'd be a match for Cadell any day. Come along, we'll have Harry contact the milk board first thing tomorrow," Gwen replied, and slipping her arm into her brother's, she smiled, glad to have him back, even as dangerous times lay ahead.

* * *

"And you're certain about this?" Harry asked, and Gwen nodded.

"The milk came from Robinson's Dairy. All the children got ill. There's no other proof needed, is there? Apart from Owain's testimony," she replied.

They had returned to the dairy, Gwen, Madlen, Bryn, and Owain. Gwen had recounted the tale of what had happened at the party, and of how her brother had agreed to testify against their uncle and cousin. Harry had been sceptical at first, but it had not taken him long to be convinced of the seriousness of what he was being told.

"It's wicked," he said, and Gwen nodded.

"But a stop can be put to it–*we* can put a stop to it," she said, and Harry nodded.

He was not a man prone to immediate action–a ponderer, rather than a doer. But it was clear he grasped the seriousness of the situation, and despite the suggestion the matter could wait until the morning, he immediately put on his hat and coat, telling them he would go to the milk board at once.

"Tell them Owain will testify and tell them Mrs. Brooks from the song school will, too. She was devastated about what happened, but it could work to our advantage. She'll tell them Robinson's Dairy sold her the milk. There's no doubt the milk came from there, and if it was filled with chalk, it's no wonder the children fell ill," Gwen said.

Harry nodded, and hurried out into the night, leaving the others with Lisette, who had listened open-mouthed to the story, shaking her head in disbelief.

"And there was I feeling jealous at not being given an invitation. Well, I'm glad I didn't go. I couldn't have resisted the trifle, but I'm glad I wasn't given the chance to," she said, glancing at Bryn, who blushed.

"I could only invite two guests," he replied, but Lisette only laughed.

"And for your sake, I'm glad neither of them ate any of the trifle, either," she replied.

Gwen smiled. She was glad, too. But the thought of the children suffering, of what might have been the case had one of them eaten more than their fair share, did not bear thinking about.

"They're lucky no one died," Madlen said, and Gwen nodded.

"No, but it easily could've happened and perhaps it already has. Do you know of anyone else who's been poisoned by the milk, Owain?" she asked, glancing at her brother, who shook his head.

"I don't know… and I don't want to know, either. If I did… I'd be responsible for it," he said, and Gwen nodded.

"Uncle Dawid might know, though, or Cadell. And back in the valley, too–all the milk they sent to London. It's too awful for words. But you've done the right thing, Owain," she said, and her brother nodded.

"I just don't know what's going to happen… later, I mean. When it's all over," Owain said.

Bryn shook his head.

"I don't know if they'll look leniently on you, Owain. It's a very serious crime, and if your Uncle Dawid can be linked…" he began, but Gwen stopped him.

"Whatever happens, you've done the right thing, Owain. I know it might not seem like that now, but it will do, and you'll be treated fairly, I'm sure," Gwen said.

She did not know what would happen to her brother, even as she could only hope he would be shown leniency in his testimony. But whatever punishment he received; Gwen was determined to stand by him.

She would not abandon him. She knew what it felt like to be abandoned, and she was not about to see her brother suffer the same fate.

"I hope so," Owain said.

"I'll make some tea, and we can cut some bread and butter, too, couldn't we?" Madlen said, and Gwen nodded.

"Yes, the Christmas party wasn't quite what any of us expected it to be, was it?" she replied, and the others shook their heads.

Madlen made a pot of tea, and Lisette cut the bread and butter. There was jam, too, and the remnants of a fruit cake bought by Harry's mother. They made a pleasant meal, even as the threat of what was to come next hung over them.

After they had finished, Bryn left to return to the song school, but not before Gwen caught him on his own, the two of them standing together in the moonlit yard.

"I'm sorry today wasn't quite what you were expecting," Bryn said, and Gwen smiled.

"No... but... in a way, I'm glad of it. Not because of what happened to the children–that was terrible. But if it hadn't happened... well, Owain wouldn't have agreed to testify, and my uncle would get away with what he's been doing for... well, who knows how long," Gwen replied.

"You're right. It was for the best. I don't think any of the children are in danger now. They'll feel unwell for a few days, but that's about it, thank goodness. No... if this puts a stop to what your uncle's been doing, we can only be thankful for it," he said, and Gwen nodded.

"Absolutely. And then I suppose... well... I'm not sure what happens next. After Christmas, and..." she began, her words faltering as tears welled up in her eyes.

She felt foolish for crying, and yet she knew just why she was doing so. This was to be their last Christmas together. Bryn would leave, and Gwen and Madlen would be left in London. It was to be a parting of ways, the Christmas services marking the end of Bryn's time at the song school. A finale to all he had achieved.

"I want you to come with me, Gwen, back to Wales, back to the farm," he said, and Gwen stared at him in astonishment.

"But... what do you mean?" she exclaimed, for the thought of doing so was too remarkable for words.

She could not simply return to the valley, or could she? The thought had crossed her mind on dozens of occasions. But to return to the farm, to return to where everything had begun…

"I mean, I'm going back. I don't know quite what I'll do, but… well, it occurred to me, if your uncle and cousin are charged with adulterating the milk, the farm would be yours. They couldn't challenge you over it. Have the milk board sign it over to you. You know more about milking and dairy herds than most people. You could farm the land, establish a new herd. We could do it together," he said, the enthusiasm building in his voice.

Gwen was astonished but delighted, too. London was not her home and living there had served only as a reminder of all she had lost. She longed for the open valley, the soaring mountains, the lush fields, and forests. But as for going back, she had always doubted the possibility, knowing her uncle still had a claim to the farm, and whilst he was still at large, the danger of his returning remained.

"Do you really think we could?" she asked, and Bryn nodded.

"I know we could, and we could do it well. Gwen. I… I don't want to leave you. I know you must think me foolish, but… I can't imagine my life without you," he said, and Gwen smiled.

"I can't imagine mine without you, either," she replied, slipping her hand into his.

For a moment, they stood in silence, gazing into one another's eyes in the moonlight. There was no doubting Gwen's feelings for Bryn. She loved him, and she could not imagine loving anyone else but him. But as for his feelings towards her, Gwen had been uncertain.

London was filled with distractions–with pretty women who found the power of his voice, attractive. But Bryn had chosen Gwen, and for that, she could only be grateful, even as it had always seemed inevitable–right from the very first moment they had met. Song had brought them together, and it had kept them together, too.

"Then it's decided?" he asked, and Gwen nodded.

"It's decided," she replied, and leaning forward, he kissed her on the cheek.

"I should be going. Don't tell Madlen just yet. I want it to be a surprise for her, too. We'll run the farm together, the three of us, and in time, your brother, too," he said, and Gwen nodded.

"I'd like that, and I know they would, too. Just a little longer," she said, and Bryn nodded.

"A little longer, yes, but soon," he replied, and with a final farewell, he headed out of the yard and back towards the song school.

Gwen watched him go, pulling her shawl tightly

around her shoulders against the cold. But the chill of the night could not overcome the warmth in her heart, and the thought of all Bryn had promised her filled her with joy.

THE ASSIZES

Gwen had gone to bed before Harry returned that night, but in the morning, when she and Madlen rose for the milking, he was waiting for them in the milking parlour.

"They're raiding Robinson's Dairy this morning, first thing," he said, and Gwen and Madlen glanced at one another nervously.

"What else did they say?" Gwen asked, for she was anxious to know what would become of Owain once the milk board had made its raid.

"I told them what happened at the song school. They'll question the cook, and as for your brother… well, that's up to the judge. He's involved in it. There's no doubting that. But as for whether he'll be punished in the same way… well, only time will tell," he said, and Gwen nodded.

Owain was still asleep. Gwen had made him up a bed in the hayloft above where the herd slept. She did not want to wake him, knowing the day would be a difficult one. But she was glad of Harry's news, and she knew it was now only a matter of waiting...

* * *

"Any news?" Bryn asked when he came from choir practice at the chapel later that morning.

Owain was now awake, and Gwen was waiting in the milking parlour with him and Madlen.

"We haven't heard anything yet. Lisette went to see what was happening, but she hasn't come back yet," Gwen replied.

They were growing impatient, and Gwen could tell Owain was nervous.

"The inspectors came to question Mrs. Brooks. She was in such a state over it, but they assured her she wasn't to blame for using the adulterated milk in the trifle," Bryn said, and Gwen nodded.

"I'm glad–it's only right, she didn't do anything wrong, did she?" she said, glancing at Owain, who shook his head.

"It was Cadell who sold it to her. He said it was the best milk money could buy. He always said so. He used to have a small churn of the best milk he could find–not with chalk in it. He'd let the customer try it then they'd buy it, of course," Owain said, shaking his head.

Gwen was about to reply, wanting to reassure him, when the sound of horse's hooves caused them all to look up out of the window. Outside, in the yard in front of the dairy, a cart had pulled up, drawn by two horses. Three men now got out, and Gwen recognised them as some of the same men who had come to the dairy previously to make a surprise inspection.

"Owain…" Gwen said, and Owain took a deep breath and rose to his feet.

"I'm going to do the right thing," he said, as a knock came at the door.

Gwen went to answer it, finding the three men on the step, one of them holding a set of papers.

"We're looking for Owain Parry," one of them said.

He was the same one who had spoken last time, and Gwen was about to step aside when Owain himself stepped forward.

"I'm Owain Parry," he replied, and the man nodded, his eyes narrowing.

"It's claimed you're willing to testify in the case against your uncle and cousin concerning adulterated milk. But I must warn you, whatever you say could be used in evidence against you, too. Your uncle and cousin claim you're involved in this as much as they are, and it seems they're willing to take you down with them if you testify," he said, but Owain shook his head.

"I was involved, but it all started when I was a child. They took me from the farm when the last set of milk inspectors came knocking. I was only ten years old," he said, and Gwen nodded.

Her brother was being brave, and Gwen could only admire him for what he was now doing. But she wanted to defend him, too, and before the milk inspector could reply, she interrupted.

"It's true. He was only a child. If anyone's at fault, it's our Uncle Dawid, even when it comes to Cadell, too. It all began after our Aunt Cerian died. Before that, Uncle Dawid was a good and honest man. But something happened, something changed. He was different after she died. Perhaps it was his way of coming to terms with his grief. But he took a dark path. I think he watered down the milk at first, then he turned to chalk. He had Cadell do it with him, then they forced Owain to join them. It wasn't his fault," she said, and the milk inspector's eyes narrowed.

"Be that as it may, you're not a child anymore, Owain. You're still culpable. But perhaps the judge will look favourably on you," he said, and Owain nodded.

"I'm ready to receive whatever punishment he

deems necessary," he said, holding out his hands in an act of surrender.

Tears welled up in Gwen's eyes, but there was nothing more she could do. Owain was taken away, and Gwen, Madlen, Bryn, and Lisette sat dejectedly in the milking parlour. All thoughts of the farm, and returning to the valley, were tinged with sadness, and the knowledge of what could become of Owain now he had been taken away.

"You'll have to testify, too–both of you, and I might have to do so, too," Bryn said.

But Gwen was only too willing to do so. She wanted to defend her brother and Madlen said the same.

"We can tell the judge what happened to us — how Uncle Dawid and Cadell treated us. He'll believe us, I'm sure," Madlen said.

"But he may still have to punish Owain nonetheless," Bryn replied.

"We can only wait and see," Gwen said, knowing the matter was now out of their hands.

She wondered what her uncle was thinking. Did he even know she and Madlen had a part to play, or did he merely think Owain had had a change of heart? She could picture the angry look on his face and that of Cadell, too. Gwen knew they would do all they could to defend themselves, and to make out someone else was to blame.

"We both have to testify, Gwen, don't we?" Madlen asked, when later they were making butter.

Gwen nodded. It seemed strange to be doing something so ordinary when their brother's future hung in the balance. But there was little else they could do, and making butter was what they always did…

"We do, yes. We must make the judge understand Owain played a lesser part in all of this than the others," she said.

"Uncle Dawid will try to make himself out as the innocent party, won't he?" Madlen said, and Gwen nodded.

"He will, yes. And Cadell will, too. But we can't let them get away with it, Madlen. We've got to be strong and then… well, there's something I want to tell you about, something Bryn said," she replied.

Madlen looked at her in surprise, and Gwen now went on to recount what Bryn had said to her about returning to Wales and running the farm together. Madlen listened intently, and when Gwen had finished, she smiled.

"So, you're getting married, are you?" she asked, and Gwen blushed.

Bryn had not proposed to her–the question had not even occurred to her. But they could not very well run the farm together, and live as he proposed without a union being enacted.

"I... well, yes, I suppose we will," she said, and Madlen smiled.

"I'm glad, Gwen. You deserve to be happy. Both of you do. You've spent so long looking after me... well, I'm pleased for you," she said, and Gwen smiled back at her.

"And you won't mind going back to Wales?" she asked.

Madlen shook her head.

"Mind? I dream of it. The deep valley, the high mountains, the lush meadows, the gushing streams... I never wanted to leave, and I'm so glad to think we can go back there," she replied, and Gwen slipped her hand into her sister's and squeezed it.

"Very soon, we can," she replied, hoping her words were not hollow, even as they still had their own mountain to climb.

* * *

"Order, order, the court will come to order. Do you hear me?" the judge called out, banging his gavel down hard on the dais, where he sat in his wig and gown, raised about the packed courtroom.

News of the adulterated milk had spread far and wide, and hundreds of people had crammed into the assize court that morning to hear the charges read against Gwen's uncle and cousin.

Gwen and Madlen were there, sitting next to Bryn, in the gallery, and now they peered down, watching as the three defendants were led in. Owain had been charged with the lesser offence of complicity in criminal undertakings and sat apart from his uncle and cousin. His hands were chained, but there was a resolute and determined look on his face, and Gwen could only admire him for what he was about to do.

"Your honour, the prosecution makes an allegation of the following crimes," the clerk said, before reading out a list of offences, including attempted poisoning.

A murmur went up around the courtroom, and the judge banged his gavel again, calling for order.

"How do the defendants plead?" he said.

"Not guilty," Gwen's uncle and cousin replied in unison, but Owain said the opposite.

"Guilty, your honour," he said, and a gasp went up around the courtroom.

One woman fainted and had to be carried out, and when the proceedings continued, the judge reminded the defendants of the seriousness of the charge.

"We'll hear testimony now from the defendants," he said, and Gwen's uncle was brought forward.

As expected, he denied all the charges vehemently, blaming Owain for being behind the plot to adulterate the milk. Cadell did the same, but when Owain himself was called to the stand, a very different tale emerged.

He told of how he had been forced into partnership with his uncle and cousin, coerced into adulterating the milk, and left with no choice but to follow where the others led. His words were compelling, and he did not attempt to deny the charges laid against him. He was brave, and Gwen was astonished at the change come over him.

"I've heard enough now," the judge said, giving no indication of whom he would choose to believe.

Mrs. Brooks was now called to the stand, where she testified as to having been sold the milk by Cadell and told it was the freshest in all of London.

"Twenty years I've been making trifles, your honour, and not once have I ever poisoned anyone. Oh, it was too terrible. I was heartbroken, those poor children. I don't think I'll ever cook again," she said, throwing her hands up in the air.

"Yes… thank you, Mrs. Brooks. I think I've heard enough from you, too," the judge said, raising his eyebrows as Mrs. Brooks retreated from the witness stand in a flood of tears.

Gwen's heart was beating fast. She knew she was next, but she did not yet know if her uncle and cousin knew she was there.

"Gwen Parry," the clerk called out.

"Good luck," Bryn whispered, and Gwen made her way down from the gallery to the courtroom, mounting the witness stand, and catching her uncle's eye as she did so.

He looked at her with a mixture of anger and surprise, as did her cousin. But Gwen held her nerve, looking back at them both defiantly.

"Tell the court, Gwen, in your own words, what you know," the judge said, and that was precisely what Gwen did.

She began at the beginning, recounting her early life on the farm, and the realisation of what her uncle and cousin were doing. She defended Owain, reminding the court he was only a child when their uncle's wickedness began.

All the while, her uncle sat silently, his eyes fixed on her. Cadell was looking down, and Gwen wondered whether he at last was feeling shame for what he had done.

"I know what they did, and I know what they're still doing. My brother had a part to play–of course, he did. But he also realised the error of his ways. I beg for leniency for him," Gwen said, as she finished giving her evidence.

"Thank you, Miss Parry. Your sister may take the stand now," the judge said, nodding at Gwen, who thanked him and returned to her seat.

She caught her brother's eye as she passed, and he smiled at her.

"Thank you," he mouthed.

"That was wonderful," Bryn whispered as Madlen took to the stand.

Gwen slipped her hand into Bryn's and squeezed it.

"I just hope it's enough," she replied.

EPILOGUE

HOME

As it turned out, it *was* enough, though Owain was still sentenced to six months hard labour and imprisonment on one of the prison hulks moored on the Thames. Their uncle and Cadell fared far worse. They were to be deported to Australia never to be heard from again.

The dairy was closed, and whilst many people had fallen ill from drinking the adulterated milk, no one could be proved to have died. Gwen was grateful the matter was over, and she was faithful in visiting her brother during his imprisonment.

She and Madlen would take food parcels to him,

and when the time came for his sentence to be over, he was welcomed home.

"It'll be strange to see him here again – I suppose it's strange for us all," Gwen said, looking out from their vantage point on Mervgyn's Rock, across the meadows and down the valley towards the village, where a plume of smoke announced the arrival of the steam train from London carrying her brother.

They liked to go to the rock together, remembering happy times, as well as sad, and looking out over the farm the milk inspectors had given to Gwen after her uncle's sentencing.

The past six months had been remarkable. Bryn had finished his studies at the song school, but instead of taking on a role in a London choir, or even on the stage, he had decided to return to the valley as he had promised.

Reverend Llewlyn and the other residents had been surprised to see the pair return, along with Madlen, and even more surprised to learn they would be farming Gwen's uncle's land.

"Bless my soul. We all thought you were gone for good," Reverend Llewlyn had said, but Gwen had only smiled and shaken her head.

"This is my home, Reverend Llewlyn. It's where I belong," she had replied.

They had been back at the farm together for a month now, and with a new herd and new labourers, things were beginning to return to what they had been when Gwen's aunt was alive. There was no question of adulterating the milk. It was fresh and delicious, and needed nothing more than to be drunk or made into butter or cheese.

Madlen saw to this, and an agreement had been reached with Harry Bartlett in London to supply the song school with products from the farm. It was everything Gwen had ever wanted, though one question remained…

"I'm still not used to being back here. I know it's where we grew up, but… well, I got so used to London, and the valleys are so peaceful, I keep expecting to see a hansom cab pull up," Bryn said, and Gwen laughed.

"But you're happy you came back?" she asked, and he nodded.

"Very happy. I wouldn't want to be anywhere else but here. And you?" he asked.

Gwen smiled.

"I wouldn't want to be anywhere else, either. I used to dream about coming back to the valleys. It was… all I ever wanted," she said, and Bryn slipped his hand into hers.

"Gwen… I've waited to say this to you… I wanted to make sure you were happy. Coming back here… leaving London. I was certain it was the right thing to do, but I didn't know if it was the right thing for both of us. Do you understand what I'm saying?" he asked, and Gwen nodded.

Her heart skipped a beat, realising what it was he was saying.

"But it is, isn't it? We belong here, in the valley, and together," she said, and Bryn smiled.

"We do, yes. And I want us to stay here, forever. And I want us to be together, forever," he said, taking her hand in his.

"And we can be. I wouldn't have it any other way," she said.

> "Gwen, may your life entirely be
> Beneath the midday sun's bright glow,
> And may a blushing rose of health
> Dance on your cheek a hundred years.
> I forget all your words of promise
> You made to someone, my pretty girl
> So give me your hand, my sweet, dear, Gwen,
> For no more but to say "farewell.""

As the song came to an end, a tear rolled down Gwen's cheek, and she smiled, gazing into Bryn's eyes, caught up in the joy of the moment they now shared. There was no doubting her love for him and his love for her, too. She wanted to spend the rest of her life with him, and it was clear he felt the same.

"I do give you my hand," she whispered, and he

smiled, leaning forward, and kissing her gently on the lips.

"Then that's all I need to know," he replied, as the shrill whistle of the steam train sounded in the valley below.

"We've got so much to look forward to," Gwen whispered, and Bryn nodded.

"So much to look forward to together," he replied.

"But won't you miss singing? In the choir, I mean," she asked, but he shook his head.

"The songs we sang weren't meant for the city, or to be held in the confines of chapel walls. They were meant to be sung in places like this, praising God from the mountain tops, just like the prophets of old," he said, rising to his feet.

Gwen stood next to him, and now, with his voice raised, he sang, singing out to the valley with all the strength of his voice. It was one of the old songs, one his grandmother had taught him, and Gwen joined in, too, knowing just what he meant as their voices carried on the fresh, mountain air.

"I love you Bryn," Gwen whispered, as the song came to an end.

"I love you, too, Gwen, with all my heart. It was song that brought us together, and I know we'll still be singing that same song for the rest of our lives," he replied, and Gwen smiled.

He was right, and the thought of doing so filled her with joy. As she looked out over the valley, Gwen knew there was nowhere she would rather be and no one else she would rather be there with. She loved him, and it was with a song of love in their hearts they would look to the future. A future filled with happiness.

The End

If you enjoyed this story, could I please ask you to leave a review on Amazon?

Thank you so much.

Printed in Great Britain
by Amazon